PRAISE FOR STACY LEE'S

THE HUNDREDTH TIME AROUND

"I could see the Nubble Lighthouse in the distance. When the characters walked through the sandy beaches falling in love or experiencing heartbreak, I, too, could hear the music wafting over from the nearby piano bar."

— ALLISON NOWAK—REEDSY

"This book earns a rating of **4 out of 4 stars**. If you enjoy a classic love story full of summer flings, heartbreaks, anxieties, sacrifices, secrets, and second chances, then you'll appreciate all that *The Hundredth Time Around* has to offer."

— AVID BIBLIOPHILE—ONLINE BOOK CLUB

"I read this book in a day, once I started I couldn't stop I had to know how the love story ends. It's beautifully written, with so many twists and turns that I never saw coming. It's a beautiful modern day love story with a classic love that makes us all long for more books by this author."

— KATIE BRESSACK—FAN

PRAISE FOR STACY LEE'S

FUTURE PLANS

In Book 2 of her Maine-set Nubble Light series, Lee offers skillful plotting that unveils several surprises readers won't see coming, both in the thriller and romance departments.

— KIRKUS REVIEW

Great read! It had my heart racing at times and tears in my eyes at other times. It had many unexpected moments I wasn't able to see coming!

— DANYELLE DICECCA- FAN

The author has a unique style of writing. She has her story development under control, no matter the twist that she adds at any point...I'd rate it **four out of four stars**. I'd recommend this book to romance lovers. The love story painted in this book was real and would interest anyone who enjoys such stories.

— ONLINE BOOK CLUB

# FUTURE PLANS

## A NOVEL

## STACY LEE

Future Plans by Stacy Lee

Copyright © 2021 by Stacy Lee

French Martini Press

Salem, New Hampshire

Cover Art- Spark Creative

Dedication and About the Author Photo- Stella Moon Photography by Jamie Valcanas

❀ Created with Vellum

*For my daughter, my friend.*

# A NOTE TO THE READER

This is the second book in the Nubble Light series. The first book, *The Hundredth Time Around*, was published in January of 2021. *Future Plans* is the second book in the series. Book three is already in the works!

The Nubble Light Series was inspired by my visit to York Beach in 2020. My mother-in-law, Shirley Barbagallo, brought me and my family to visit during what ended up being some of the last months of her life. During this visit, we fell in love with the beaches of York, Maine, as well as Cape Neddick and the Nubble Lighthouse. Because of this, the Nubble Lighthouse will always hold a special place in my heart.

Also, please be on the lookout for a special mini-series I am writing for elementary-aged children from the point of view of dogs at day care. Please visit www. frenchmartinipress.com or check out Facebook for more information!

# ACKNOWLEDGMENTS

I would like to once again thank Lynn and her team at Red Adept Editing. I couldn't do it without you! Also, another huge thanks to Julie and her team at Spark Creative for designing my cover. You did it again! Thank you for taking the time to listen to my ideas. Your attention to detail and creativity have been nothing short of fantastic.

Thank you to Kris and the team at the Talking Book. Collaborating with you and your team on the audiobook for *The Hundredth Time Around* was an incredible experience. I can't wait to bring the characters from *Future Plans* to life with you.

Thank you to my husband, Paul Barbagallo. Not only do you encourage and motivate me to live my dreams, but I could never write about true love and what it really means without experiencing it with you. I love you with all my heart, and I thank God each day for you. Thank you for being such a supportive husband and amazing father.

Thank you to an incredible mother-in-law, Shirley Barbagallo. Not a day goes by that we don't think of you and remember how much you loved us. Thank you for taking me to the Nubble Lighthouse that summer. My world has been forever changed. I wrote this entire book underneath the warmth of your giving shawl, Ma. Thank you for keeping me toasty warm on these cold winter New England days.

Also, a huge thank you to my children, Paul and Lucy. One of these days I am going to write a book that you are allowed to read, I promise. I am inspired by the way you have both overcome the challenges you have endured over the past year. Even though cheerleading and basketball days are behind us right now, you have focused your energy on new dreams and goals. Keep dreaming big and never give up. You are what you believe.

Thank you to my aunt, Patricia Fishwick, and my parents, Dan and Karen DeBruyckere, for talking with me about life in 1970. I wish I could go back in time and experience it with you! I love you all very much.

Thank you to my friends and family—my biggest cheerleaders! My parents, Karen and Daniel DeBruyckere, my sister, Kate Giglio, my sister-in-law, Cheri Grassi, and my friend, Lauren Strob. Writers can only write what we know, and I have you all to thank for teaching me what it means to truly love.

Thank you Stacie Swanson for encouraging me. I appreciate your friendship and am thankful for your help with editing. I can't wait for our cruise in 2022!

Thank you Marisa and Josh Berlin for our family vacations over these past couple of months. Thank you, Marisa, for listening to my ideas and for believing in me. Like I said, we are going to make the best old ladies someday (all we need is our shawls, fireplace, and martinis).

To my best friend, Kara Holloway, thank you for standing by me and supporting me and for reminding me each day without even having to say a word that you are proud of me. You really are the best friend a person could ever ask for. I am so glad that Paul and I get to do life with you, Court, and the kids.

To my little brother, Dan, we love you no matter what, and we are blessed to have you in our lives. We are here for you, always.

Thank you to the community of York Beach, Maine, and the Cape Neddick community. You have been so receptive to the Nubble Light Series, and it warms my heart to know you have enjoyed my stories. Thank you to the Union Bluff Hotel and Event center for not only providing us with memorable vacations but for continuing to serve as the perfect setting in the Nubble Light Series.

Of course, I need to thank you, the reader! Thank you for reading my novels and for all of your feedback. It brings such joy to my heart that you are falling in love with the characters just as I have. May you continue to love without hesitation and keep all of your relationships tucked away in a safe place. Always remember these memories: Past, present, and future… and lean on them to warm your heart during difficult times. I hope you enjoy book two of the Nubble Light Series. Thank you and God Bless!

# PROLOGUE

## IN THE FUTURE

She stands at the door in anticipation. After all, she has only waited her entire life for this night. Everything is perfect, what she has always imagined it would be, knowing that now, after all this time, *she* will be the one smiling in the pictures and *she* will be the one dancing in the spotlight. It is nothing short of a dream come true. She has envisioned it many times: her arms wrapped around him tightly, their feet moving together in unison to her favorite song. She imagines the smiles on their faces as they watch in admiration, knowing that happily ever after does exist. She knows because she is living it. She has sat back and watched, time after time, other people living their dreams... so it seems only right that now, after all this time, it is her turn to live, her turn to love.

She presses her lips together and closes her eyes. Her stomach flips and flops, and her heart races, faster and faster like a beat of a drum, picking up at a steady pace and building dynamically. Any minute now, she will open the door. She will step over the threshold, and he will be on the other side. He will take her hand in his. He will smile in that familiar way he does, nothing short of perfect.

The night won't last forever, and this saddens her. But when the last song ends and the dance floor clears... it will be only the beginning. They will walk out together, hand in hand. Not just into the perfect sunset but into a life full of love and a future full of promise... just as she had always planned.

IN THE PAST- EMILINE 1971

CHAPTER ONE

*T*he Nubble Lighthouse. Just when I thought I had seen it all. The spectacular colors of the green gardens in Paris, France. The wonders of the Rocky Mountains in Colorado. The crystal-clear night sky of Yarmouth, Nova Scotia; so clear, in fact, that I believed I could reach up and pluck a twinkling star from outer space with my bare hands if I tried. I was blessed to have traveled to so many places at such a young age, fortunate enough to experience the authenticity of many different countries and cultures. But this setting, this place, it was breathtaking. The lighthouse had appeared miniature to the naked eye at first, but upon studying the way it towered over me up on the hill, its rocky coastline and lifelike waves that crashed one after another, the way it reflected the golden sun as it started to rest, specks of pink and purple glistening back at me on that evening, an overwhelming sense of inspiration took over, and I allowed myself to dream.

I had never been much of a dreamer. It was a rare occasion that I allowed myself to get too attached to any one place. My father was a pilot. He flew the new and improved

3

jumbo jets that only recently became popular about a year ago. Although I loved flying around with my parents and seeing the world, I sometimes longed for a normal life. Of course, at twenty-three years old, I could have suggested that I stay back home in London, alone. After all, I had friends and family there; I had a life. But there was something about traveling to new places that I couldn't resist. And it was moments like this, when Mother Nature met the power of man, and landmarks like this lighthouse reminded me that anything was possible, that deep in my heart, I knew there was something special waiting for me. My imagination overtook the power of my rationality, and the quiet prison I sometimes created for myself would just melt away. It was times like this when I felt as though I was home.

I placed my blanket over the rocky ground beneath me and sat down. I crossed my legs and pulled my skirt over my knees. The blank canvas appeared clean and fresh as I retrieved it out of my bag. I found my pencil and my oil pastels and placed them down in front of me, all the while keeping my eyes focused on the masterpiece that stood before me, the tiny lighthouse and its little piece of Earth. It had been my intention to sketch the lighthouse first and then come back another night to shade in my creation. I couldn't resist the way the delicate colors danced above me, so I decided that I would need to capture all of these magnificent elements tonight. I would need to start working quickly before it got dark, as my father would be very unhappy if I didn't return to the Anderson Cottage prior to nightfall, and I didn't have much time.

"Are you a famous artist or something?"

My shoulders tightened at the sound of the stranger's voice. I jumped to my feet and glanced down the cliff toward the large mountain of rocks. A young man, who looked to be my age, was climbing up them toward me. It wasn't until then that I also noticed a group of people, about fifty yards to my right, perched on the rocks, bottles of beer in hand.

"I like to paint," I replied. "But I'm not sure I would consider myself to be an artist."

He made his way over to where I was sitting. "Can I sit here?" he asked, like he had known me for years. He was dressed more appropriately for a night out, not a night on the beach. His tan polyester leisure suit stood no chance against the brown soil at my feet.

I smirked. "Aren't you worried about ruining your trousers?"

"My trousers?" He laughed. "You mean my pants?"

"Yes, your fancy pants," I affirmed. "If you sit here, with me on this ground, you are sure to ruin your fancy trousers."

He laughed, and when he did, his brown mustache seemed to take on a life of its own. He chuckled and ran his fingers through his brown hair. "Not if I sit on that," he said, pointing to the navy-blue blanket I had borrowed from the Anderson Cottage.

"Well, all right, then," I agreed. "Have a seat." I sat back down and stretched my blanket out as far as it could go. He sat down next to me. He smelled like cigarettes and beach air.

"Looks good," he said as he studied my sketch.

"Well, I didn't get very far." I sighed.

"Why is that?"

"Well, you came along, for starters."

He crossed his arms over his chest. "I can take a hint," he said, his eyebrows raising slightly. He began to stand back up, but I placed my hand on his arm.

"You don't have to go," I said, realizing for a quick beat that I really didn't want him to leave. "Are those your friends down there, getting pissed?"

"Pissed?"

I laughed. "Drunk," I explained. "Where I come from, we call it getting pissed."

He laughed, and it sounded like music to my ears. I studied him closely and considered the possibility that underneath his shaggy brown hair and trendy mustache, there might have simply been a real person under there who just wanted to talk.

"Yes, those are my friends. This has always been... kind of where we hang out," he explained. He gestured toward the small hangout. A girl who looked a tad bit younger than me was sitting on the ground with her acoustic guitar on her lap. Her voice echoed through the night air. It was soft and angelic. I struggled to make out the song she sang, but it was difficult. I brushed off the sudden and unexpected urge to be a part of it.

My eyes grew wide, and I studied him carefully. "Well, are *you* getting pissed?" I asked, a small giggle escaping from somewhere inside me.

"Me? Drunk?"

"Yes, you. Pissed."

"No, but I can. I mean, can I get you a drink?"

"Me? Heavens no. If I came back smelling like booze, my father would have my head." I ran my finger horizontally across my throat to signify my inevitable beheading.

He laughed. "Well, we wouldn't want that," he replied, his tone turning serious.

"No, we wouldn't," I agreed. A slight chill ran through me, and I shuddered. It was remarkable how quickly the air turned cool here. I rubbed my arms in an attempt to ease the prickliness of the goose bumps that were forming on my bare skin.

"Are you cold?" he asked.

"Yes," I confessed. "Just a bit."

"Want my jacket?"

I thought about it for a moment. "You don't even know me. Why would you want to give me your jacket?" I asked, making an effort to remind him that we had only just met.

His eyes found mine. The playfulness of the moment faded away, like the end of a romantic scene at a major motion picture. "You're right," he affirmed. "I don't know you, but I would love the chance to try."

"Try?"

"To get to know you."

I smiled and met his stare. The blue in his eyes reminded me of the way the dark colors of the ocean had hypnotized me just moments earlier. Now, this person... this stranger and his ocean-blue eyes had me feeling just as captivated. "Sure," I whispered.

"Sure?" he asked, confused. "You want to get to know me?"

"No." I snickered. "I will take your jacket."

He exhaled, and I realized he had been holding his breath in anticipation of my response. He removed his jacket and placed it around my shoulders. I slipped one arm in at a time, growing fond of the smell of him. I reached under the back of the sport coat and pulled my long blond hair through the top and collected it over my shoulders. I closed the jacket over me and hugged my arms to my chest. I recognized the smell of his aftershave. "Old Spice," I declared. "Very nice choice."

He folded his arms over his chest. "I'm impressed."

"Nothing gets by this nose," I bragged. I pointed to my nose and laughed to myself, thinking of my father's love for Old Spice. My mother gifted it to him in his Christmas stocking year after year.

"I guess not," he agreed. He moved closer to me on the blanket, and my knees grew weak. His arm brushed up against mine. "What's your name anyways?" he asked.

I smiled, thankful that he finally asked. "You tell me yours first," I insisted.

"Why is that?" he asked, pretending to nudge my arm.

"Because," I started, "if you tell me first, then I can tell you mine, and you won't be a stranger."

"True again." He laughed. "Jason," he said. "Jason Davis."

"It's nice to meet you, Jason." I hadn't meant to whisper. But for some reason, I was suddenly incapable of forming words in the way I intended. He was closer now, and if I wanted to, I could rest my head on his shoulder—and I wanted to. "My name is Emiline. Emiline Wilson." I extended my hand out to him for a handshake, but instead of shaking my hand, he pressed it to his mustache and kissed it. The bristles of his whiskers tickled my fingers.

"Well aren't you just the ladies' man?" I giggled.

"No, just a gentleman," he insisted, which was something I could already sense about him.

I pulled my hand back and fiddled with my pencil. "Your friend has a beautiful voice," I said, gesturing to where his friends were seated.

He nodded. "That's Beverly," he explained. "You will never see her without that guitar on her lap. Beverly is my buddy John's kid sister."

I listened again and this time could hear a familiar Joan Baez tune. I wondered if someday, when I would be old and gray, I would think of Jason Davis each time I heard it. I quickly shook away the thought. "Do you live here?" I asked, trying desperately to control the pounding in my chest.

"Yes, ma'am," he replied. "Right here in Cape Neddick. I graduated a few years back. I've been bartending downtown ever since. How about you? Are you here on vacation?"

"You could say that," I started. "My whole life is sort of a vacation in a way."

"How so?" he asked as his hand moved closer to mine.

"My father is a pilot."

"Like, in the air force?"

"No, just a pilot. He flies the 747 jumbo jets," I explained. "My parents love to travel, so my father's job is their ticket. I'm along for the ride, I guess you could say."

"Groovy!" he exclaimed.

I turned to study him once again. I wondered what his smile would look like underneath the mop of fuzzy hair on his upper lip. From what I could tell, it was quite nice. His mustache was so... I don't know... unfortunate. "Yes, groovy," I repeated. My accent made the word seem generic and out of place.

"Where are you from?" he asked.

"My accent doesn't give it away?"

"Well, you obviously aren't from New England."

"I stick out like a sore thumb, don't I?"

His smile turned serious, and he studied me for a beat. "I think it's beautiful, your accent." His voice trailed off into the night.

It was dark now, and my father was sure to be furious. I wondered if he had already sent out a search party. I blushed. "London. London, England," I said, glancing down at my watch. "So, Jason from Cape Neddick, Maine... it's getting late." I started to gather my things, but he placed his hand on my arm. The warmness that ran through my veins was invigorating, and the last thing I wanted to do was leave. It wasn't my usual behavior to befriend strangers. It especially wasn't typical of me to feel so connected to one.

He seemed to sense it, too, and he pressed my hand to his lips once more. "I'm glad I met you," he whispered.

"I'm glad I met you too."

His eyes locked on mine, and I was torn between what felt appropriate and what felt right. He reached forward and kissed the top of my forehead. I closed my eyes and envisioned standing up and walking down to his party with him, hand in hand. He would introduce me to his friends, and I would join their circle. We would sit together, Jason and I, listening to the angelic voice of Beverly and the sweet sound of her guitar. I would rest my head on his shoulder, and he would sing into my ear. I could see it so clearly and wanted it so badly that I almost believed it to be true. But it wasn't. And the reality was that in just two short weeks, I would be flying home to London, and I would be leaving Jason Davis behind. "I... I have to go," I said. I stood. "Can I have my blanket back? I borrowed it from the cottage I am staying at."

"Of course." He stood, reached down, and collected the blanket. He brushed it off against his leg and then handed it to me. I hugged the soft fabric to my chest.

I turned to leave but stopped in my tracks. "Bloody hell, your jacket!" I exclaimed. "I almost took it with me."

"You take it," he insisted.

"I can't." I laughed. "It matches your fancy pants." I started to take it off but winced in pain. My hair had gotten stuck in one of the buttons. "Ouch," I cried. "My hair is stuck."

"Let me look."

I held the jacket in my hands and leaned my head close to him. He worked quickly and, without much effort, was able to untangle the few tresses from the wrath of his button.

"Thank you," I whispered.

He tucked the rescued strands of blond behind my ear, and his eyes grew serious. "You really are beautiful, Emiline."

I blushed and looked away. "It was really nice to meet you, Jason." I turned and started to walk away, ready to leave him and his trendy tan leisure suit and his hip group of friends behind.

"Where are you staying?" he called from where I left him.

I stopped and turned back around and considered giving him the address. I could tell him where I was living, and there was a chance we would meet again. I could lie and tell him that I was unsure of the address. I could also tell him that I didn't share that sort of thing with men I didn't know, which would in fact have been the truth. But as I stared back at him and examined the genuine way he looked at me, I couldn't help myself. Maybe it was the way the moon reflected off the water and shone on him like a spotlight, moving me in such a way that made me want to paint his portrait. Maybe it was the way he had kissed my forehead; I had never been kissed so gently. Whatever it was, I knew I was falling, fast. I needed to see him again. "The Anderson Cottage," I whispered. "Anderson Cottage, third floor." I adjusted my bag on my shoulder and hurried up the hill, eagerly anticipating our next encounter, already dreaming of what was yet to come.

## IN THE PRESENT- HAZEL

## CHAPTER TWO

*I* curse under my breath as the heat from the leather seat scalds my legs. I make a mental note to steer clear of a color that attracts the southern Florida sun next time I purchase a car. Although the discomfort of a minuscule burn seems insignificant in comparison to owning my dream car, a royal-blue 2018 Ford Mustang convertible with black interior. Standard transmission, obviously. I only drive stick.

I take a sip of my water and start my car, confirming with myself that my automobile is in fact perfect. I close the top of the car and crank the air conditioner. Even though I have lived in southern Florida for the past fourteen years, I find that I still have difficulties with the humidity and heat, especially this time of year. When I first moved down south for college, I was so overwhelmed by the temperature that I almost moved home freshman year. Air-conditioning was the only thing that kept me from fleeing back up north. There were times I had felt as though I was roasting in an Instant Pot, simmering from the inside out.

"Dial Franny," I order my Bluetooth.

Franny picks up after one ring. "Hi, Hazel," she sings with her usual peppiness.

"How is it going on the Peterson wedding cake?" I ask.

"I'm good. How are you?" she jokes.

"I'm sorry, Franny." I chuckle. "How are you?"

"Great. Thanks for asking." She laughs. "How was your date last night?"

My shoulders tighten in response to her question. "Not conversation worthy," I respond. Images of my evening flash through my mind. It wasn't completely lousy, just nothing to write home about.

"I see." She sighs. "Not your dream guy?"

"Nope," I respond. "Can I have an update on the Peterson cake, though? I'm trying to get home for Ellie's game, but there are just too many things I still need to confirm before the weekend."

"I will have it finished tonight, and I will deliver it to the venue on Saturday morning," she confirms.

"You're the best," I say, shifting into fifth gear on the highway.

"Anytime! Tell Ellie good luck at her game."

I press the phone button on my steering wheel and end the call, shifting gears again. I am thankful for Franny and her cake business. Of course, I appreciate all of my vendors, but Franny literally takes the cake when it comes to desserts. She was my roommate for all four years of college, and if it wasn't for her support and confidence in me, I might have run back home to Maine before graduation. Now, I own one of the most successful event-planning companies in the region.

I turn the stereo up and find my favorite song on my playlist, quickly passing the car in front of me. I am only ten minutes from home. Surely I will have time to make Ellie's game. My ten-year-old daughter is one of the girliest girls around, but when she takes the flag football field with her team, she never ceases to amaze me. The boys on the team have nicknamed her *Lightning*, and I don't think she minds that name one bit.

My phone rings and interrupts my thoughts. "Events by Hazel. This is Hazel Lavigne."

"Hazel, it's Dale calling from Floral Inspirations. I'm afraid I have bad news about the flowers for the Peterson wedding."

*No, you don't,* I think. There will be no bad news about the arrangements we talked about and contracted months ago. No bad news regarding the coral and pink arrangement of oriental lilies, along with the green monstera leaves with white orchids. The flowers for Melissa Peterson's wedding are nonnegotiable. She has a dream and a vision, and I bring it to life. That is why I am successful. So, Dale from Floral Inspirations, there will be no bad news.

I press my lips together in anticipation. "What's going on?"

"I'm afraid there was a mix-up with our order, and we don't have what we need for tomorrow."

I feel my cheeks grow pink, and I turn up the air conditioner. "What exactly didn't come in?" I try to stay calm, but it really pisses me off when details and plans that have been contracted for months fall through last minute.

"The lilies… and the orchids," he starts. "We have them out for order next week. I'm so sorry."

I clear my throat. "Dale," I say. "We have a contract, a *binding agreement.* I am going to need you to help me get my hands on an assortment of pink and coral oriental lilies and white orchids."

"I'm sorry, Miss Lavigne." He sounds like he is trying to catch his breath. "There is just nothing I can do."

"Dale, I understand the situation is out of your control,

but I'm not going to let you off the hook here. Falling apart on me now is completely unacceptable. I will be at your store in twenty minutes. Put your thinking cap on, Dale. This is going to be a long night."

* * *

OF COURSE, I don't make it to Ellie's game. Dale and I end up making the trip to Miami to retrieve the missing flowers. Surely he will be up all night putting the arrangements together. By the time I pull up to the security guard post at the entrance of my gated community, it is well past ten o'clock at night.

"Late night for you, ma'am," Gus states. Gus has been the security guard at the entrance to my neighborhood since Ellie and I moved in five years ago. I appreciate Gus and his desire to make small talk. Honestly though, all I want to do is make myself a martini and get to bed.

"Yup," I reply. I wait for him to open the gate so I can go home.

"Ellie scored three touchdowns today!" he exclaims.

I smile. My Ellie is a beast on the football field. She is tiny but quick on her feet. "Awesome," I sing. *Now, can you please open the gate?*

"Have a great night, Ms. Lavigne."

"You too, Gus."

The gate opens, and I drive through my neighborhood. I pass the small lake on my right that Ellie and I fell in love with when we first came to see the house. The light from the moon reflects on the water, and I pause to appreciate the serenity I find in quiet moments. Sometimes I feel as though life is happening so fast around me. I know that I am successful in my career, and that I am very accomplished for a woman in her early thirties. But there have been times when I feel like I am moving faster than the speed of light, and I can't help but anticipate a crash.

I turn down my street and drive underneath the weeping willow trees that line the road. They border both sides of the street and lean into each other, creating a tunnel-like appearance. Ellie once asked me why they are called weeping willows. "Are they sad?" she had asked. "Weeping means sad, doesn't it?" She was always thinking, that Ellie.

My response had left a lot to be desired. "Maybe you can look that up when you get to school," I had suggested.

*　*　*

BY THE TIME I get inside, eat dinner, and begin getting settled for bed, it is well past midnight. The house has been cleaned up from dinner, and Ellie and Gabrielle are already both in their rooms fast asleep. The house is so quiet that it is almost eerie.

Gabrielle, or Gabby for short, is my live-in nanny. She has been with us since Ellie was a year old. Being a single mom has not been an easy feat, to say the least. When I got pregnant with Ellie, it was my senior year of college. My parents begged me to come home and live with them. I was stubborn and determined to start my company myself. Day care was helpful, but when Events by Hazel really started to take off, I began missing pickup deadlines and pediatrician appointments, feeding fast food to my daughter for at least two of her meals every day. There were nights I cried myself to sleep, thinking that I really would not be able to do this. I never had huge plans of becoming a mother. Once I had Ellie, I struggled to fit in with other moms. I had the utmost respect and appreciated those who were able to hop on Pinterest and brainstorm ways to pack their child's healthy lunches or the moms who organized the playgroups and car pools. It just wasn't natural for me. My business was reviewed as being in the top ten event-planning companies by the time Ellie was eleven months old. Balancing my career and my daughter had started to feel impossible.

It was Franny who suggested I hire a nanny. The two of us together found Gabrielle, and she was, in fact, a dream come true. I am pretty sure that Ellie thinks of her as a mother, too, which sometimes hits a funny nerve and sometimes is almost a relief. Gabrielle is responsible for mostly everything when it comes to Ellie. I am thankful for the school lunches she packs and for all the drop-offs, pickups, and transportation to activities. Gabrielle is actually the reason that Ellie started taking an interest in football in the first place. The two of them always have a football game on the TV, and they hoot and holler at the players regardless of what game they are watching.

I finish brushing my teeth and pull my dark hair up into a messy bun. I stare at my reflection. I sigh and reach for my eye cream. Dark circles peek out underneath my blue eyes. I would need to get some sleep for the big day tomorrow. "Miss Peterson better be very happy with her floral arrangements," I say out loud. I turn off the light and get into bed, almost falling asleep before my head hits my pillow.

# IN THE PRESENT- ELLIE

## CHAPTER THREE

*I* strongly dislike fractions. I would say that I "hate" them, but my mother has told me that hate is a very strong word. The truth is though, that I really hate fractions, so I feel like I should be able to say that. My math teacher, Mrs. Freeman, says that it will get easier. She also says that it is important that I learn them now, or it will only get harder later on. She is probably right, but I would much rather be reading a book right now instead of watching my classmates take their turn one by one at the interactive whiteboard at the front of the room. I reach in my desk and pull out my glasses. You would think that being able to see the board better would help, but it doesn't.

"Eleanor," Mrs. Freeman starts. "You can solve problem number thirteen."

I swear in my mind, even though I know that it's bad to swear. I blame the fractions. Stupid. Fractions.

I walk awkwardly up to the board and look at the addition problem, fractions with unlike denominators. My cheeks grow warm, and I feel beads of sweat forming beneath my armpits. Gabby said that I should start wearing deodorant. I should have listened to her.

"Lightning," a voice calls in a whisper. Two feet behind me, sitting at his desk, is Jamison Perez. Jamison is the quarterback on the Sharks, my flag football team. He is the one who threw the three flawless passes yesterday that resulted in my touchdowns. He's the one who made up my nickname, Lightning. He is also the boy I have had a crush on since the second grade.

"What?" I whisper, feeling the heat rise to my cheeks.

He glances down at a piece of paper on his desk. He has turned it to face me. I look over at the teacher and back at him again. I can almost read his mind, as I often do on the football field. He has completed the math problem and is showing me the answer. I squint down at his paper, thankful I am wearing my glasses, and copy his work onto the board at the front of the class.

"Thank you," I say and head back to my seat.

* * *

I WAIT my turn in the parent pickup line as I do every day. I lean against the wall of the school and wait for my name to be called. Sometimes I get annoyed that they call it the *parent* pickup line. It isn't my *parent* who actually picks me up. My nanny, Gabby, gets me every day. I stare into the distance and see her silver car approaching. 3:07 p.m. on the dot. I can tell it's her because her license plate is easy to spot. Mom says that she would never want anything like that, but it suits Gabrielle. The orange, white, and green Florida plate reads DOLFINS, as she lives for the Miami Dolphins. When I asked her why she had to spell dolphins incorrectly, she explained that she was only allowed seven digits on her license plate. She is really the coolest.

"Eleanor Lavigne!" a teacher shouts.

I line up obediently at the cone. I see Gabby in the front seat waving to me. Her curly blond hair reminds me of tiny Slinkys, bouncing in all directions, as she waves hello. I get in the front seat and close the door behind me. I place my backpack on my lap and buckle my seat belt. Gabby lets me sit in the front seat even though mom doesn't like it.

"How was school?" she asks.

"Okay." I twirl a strand of my blond hair around my finger.

"Just okay?"

"Fractions," I mumble under my breath.

"I see," she replies. "We can work on them when we get home."

*Sounds like fun,* I think, sarcastically of course. I quickly make a list in my mind of ways to get out of math homework. My eyes grow wide, as if I just had the best idea in the entire world. "Can we get ice cream?" I plead.

"Ice cream?" She laughs.

"It's so hot out today, Gabby. Please?"

Gabby laughs. "Okay, ice cream first and fractions second."

"Thank you!" I squeal. I won't be able to avoid math entirely, but ice cream will definitely take the edge off. *I have the best nanny in the entire world,* I think.

\* \* \*

LATER THAT NIGHT, I am tucked in bed with my favorite elephant stuffy. My stomach starts to hurt. I was hoping that when Mommy was finished with her big wedding last week that she might start coming home earlier. She had mentioned before school this morning that the wedding was a huge success, but she still has a few other big events that require her full attention. She explained that this week she would try to get to one of my football games.

I love football. I was only playing during the fall, but I convinced my mom to sign me up for a full-year team at the sports center. Only the really good players get picked for that, so you can imagine how excited I was. I am the only girl on the team. People ask me all the time if that bothers me. I still don't understand why this would be an issue. Girls can do anything boys can do, after all. I haven't told anyone yet, but when I go to middle school, I am going to try and play tackle football. I am quick on my feet, and once I catch that football, it is really hard to stop me. I say a prayer every night that Mom will say yes.

I have another secret too. Sometimes I play a make-believe game in my mind that I have a dad. A real dad who picks me up from school, watches my football games, brings me out to dinner, and tucks me in at night. Every year at school, there is a dumb father-daughter dance. I have never been. The teachers have urged me to bring a special friend or a grandparent to the dance, but I don't bother. Gabby and I usually go to the movies or to the park and play catch on those nights. We have fun, but it would be so much better if I could just have a dad. If I had a dad, then maybe Mommy wouldn't need to work so much. Some of my friends just have a mom or just a dad. Some have both. None of them combined seem to work as much as my mother.

# IN THE PRESENT- HAZEL

## CHAPTER FOUR

*I* take a sip of my martini and glance around the bar. It is packed for a weeknight. Every table around me is filled with groups of people, eating and drinking, talking and laughing. This has become a favorite spot for Franny and me to meet up after work, when the stars align perfectly and the universe allows. The place is hopping tonight. To my left are a man and a woman who are clearly on a first date. I laugh to myself as I hear pieces of their conversation. He has inquired about her age, and she is not impressed by his question. To my right is an empty seat and a martini with Franny's name on it. If she doesn't get here soon, I might drink hers too.

As if on cue, Franny enters the bar. She is easy to spot as the color of the week for the tips of her straight blond hair is a bright, eye-popping magenta pink. "Hey!" She waves from the door. She approaches, and I am immediately jealous of the way she wears her dress. She turns the heads of many men as she approaches the bar, including the guy on the first date. I say a silent prayer for him that his date doesn't notice his obvious indiscretion.

"Sorry I'm late," she apologizes. She is sipping her martini before she removes her black Michael Kors purse from her shoulder.

"How are you?" I ask.

"I'm good! I had a fight today with some chocolate fondant, but other than that, living the dream," she jokes. She signals to the bartender. "I've got next round!" she hollers. He nods, and she turns back to me. "How's Ellie?"

I sip my martini. "She's good," I say. "I feel like I haven't seen her in ages."

"Thank God for Gabrielle," she says.

"Yes," I agree. Although I can't ignore the feeling that is growing in the pit of my stomach. *Mom guilt,* I think. Even now, sitting here over martinis with my friend, I feel guilty. But in the same breath, I know I need this time with Franny to decompress. "Gabby really is a lifesaver."

Franny nods and looks past my shoulder. "Don't look now but a really hot guy just walked in."

Of course, I turn and look, immediately causing Franny to laugh hysterically.

"You are the least patient person I know," she complains.

I smile and pretend to be listening to her, but the truth is that she is not wrong about him. He is really cute. His light-blond hair reminds me of the sand on a southern Florida beach. His round dark eyes make eye contact with mine, and for a moment, I can sense something familiar about him. He walks over to a table filled with what I assume to be a group of his friends and sits down, loosening his tie and already making small talk. "I guess he's cute," I say, trying to keep my enthusiasm to a minimum.

"Ugh, Hazel. We need to find you a guy before you turn forty."

"Oh yeah?" I laugh. "What about you?"

She waves her hand as if to say she isn't interested. "I'm

way too busy with work," she states. "Plus, I have you. I don't need anybody else."

* * *

ABOUT AN HOUR LATER, we are both three martinis deep, and we are contemplating calling an Uber to pick us up. Just as we are about to open the Uber app and hitch our rides home, Franny stares at me, eyes wide, and nods her head in a way that tells me to turn around. I realize immediately that the hot guy from earlier has shimmied his way past the crowd and is sitting to my left. I turn and acknowledge him with a smile.

"Can I buy you ladies a drink?" he asks.

Franny has had too many martinis to be on her best behavior, and I know this before she even speaks. "You can buy *her* one," she instructs.

I smirk at her and chew on my lip. "How nice of you, Franny."

She is hysterically laughing, and I shake my head. She hasn't changed since the day I met her.

"You're welcome," she says with a wink.

"I'm Russ," he says. I'm pretty sure he is trying to shake my hand.

I smile and nod in return and then turn to my phone and look at the time. It's way too late for another drink.

Franny decides to speak for me. "Russ, this is Hazel."

"It's nice to meet you, Russ." I extend my hand, and he takes it in his. I pull my hand back and press my glass to my lips and sip the final drops of my drink without taking my eyes off Russ. There is something so familiar about him, and it catches me off guard. For an instant, my breath catches in my throat. Is it his smile? The way it is a little crooked when he laughs? His eyes are dark and give off a worldly and sophisticated vibe, but his baby face contradicts that entirely. *I have met this person before*, I think. Is it the smell of his cologne? I conclude I probably have met him at one of the events I have planned. I have planned countless events: weddings, corporate. You name it, and I've organized it.

"So, what are guys drinking tonight?" he asks.

"French martinis," Franny answers, already flagging down the bartender.

"Ah, french martinis." He nods. "Can I get these two beautiful ladies another round?" he asks. "And I will take a vodka sunrise."

My heart stops beating for a moment, and for a second, I am stunned by his words. *Vodka sunrise.* It isn't often I am caught off guard, but here I am, almost at a loss for words. Almost. "Russ," I begin. "Did you go to college in Lakeland, Florida?" It isn't a long shot because it is a neighboring city, and now that I have put two and two together, I begin to piece him to a memory I would prefer to forget.

"You need to excuse her; she has had too much to drink," Franny explains as if she is my mother.

I wave her off. "No, I'm fine," I argue.

"No, I didn't, but I know people who did," he replies. "I used to party there on weekends at the frat houses." He studies me with a speck of confusion in his eyes, and I realize that he doesn't remember who I am. But pieces of that night flood my brain like tidal waves, and martinis or not, there is no doubt in my mind that I have met this Leonardo DiCaprio look-alike before. I know this because all it took was a one-time encounter for him to knock me up, disappear, and leave me pregnant with my daughter.

My legs grow weak, and I can't help but study his face like I am cramming for an exam. I try to focus, but it's hard. I tell myself that I am wrong. But I can't help but notice that although Ellie and I share a strong resemblance, she has his smile and his coloring. I try so hard to think back to that night, but my memory is foggy. So much so that I've constantly convinced myself that I wouldn't be able to pick Ellie's father out of a lineup if I tried. So why would I recognize him now? I decide again that I am incorrect in my assumptions, but a piece of me is curious, and I continue making small talk with him long enough to ask him for his business card. He hands it over eagerly, a little too eagerly. *Down, boy*, I think.

**Russell Cooper**
**Cooper Finances**
**Hollywood, Florida**

"Thanks Russell," I say. I open my purse and file his business card away in my wallet. I also decide to file him away in the *people I never want to think about again* part of my brain.

"Hey, Franny," I sing. "I think it's about time to get that Uber."

CHAPTER FIVE

"Can I borrow your green halter top?"

I turned to see my best friend standing in the doorway of my bedroom, wearing only a denim miniskirt and a strapless bra.

"You know where it is," I answered. I turned away and continued applying my makeup.

"Want me to curl your hair?" she asked as she rummaged through my closet and pulled out one of my favorite emerald-green halters. She pulled it on over her head, and I sighed. Franny always wore my clothes better than I ever could. For someone so tiny and petite, she sure had been blessed in the breast department. I didn't hate my body. It was just that my athletic shape left my chest area a lot to be desired, especially compared to my best friend.

She left my room and came back with her curling iron. After plugging it in, she hurried into the kitchen, returning with two bottles of beer. "I'm so excited for tonight!" she shrieked. "It's going to be nothing short of amazing."

\* \* \*

27

FRANNY WASN'T WRONG. The party at the Kappa Beta house was hopping. It was spring fling senior year, and people were there to party. I walked into the house, locked arm in arm with my best friend. My brunette hair was curled to perfection, thanks to Franny. Aside from curling my hair, I had also allowed her to touch up my makeup, something she had been asking to do for our entire time in undergrad, and she picked out my outfit. Low-rise denim skinny jeans and a strapless white tube top. I felt like I was on top of the world. We had already had our share to drink upon our arrival. Then, once we paid our five bucks each and were admitted into the party, we were offered Jell-O shots. We accepted and toasted to our upcoming graduation. The red substance felt slimy as it made its way down.

"Okay," Franny said. "The other girls should be here soon, but let's go scope out the area before they get here."

I laughed, as it would be just like Franny to be the first one to mark her territory. "Okay," I agreed and followed her. The music was loud, and the voices of drunk and rowdy college kids competed with the volume, causing them to shout to hear each other. We walked into the kitchen where guys were taking shots off an ice luge and passed the living room where a group of friends was already engaged in an intense game of flip cup. Franny's expression was serious as she scoped out the scene and finally settled on heading downstairs in the basement to watch some friends play beer pong. It only took ten minutes before my name was on the whiteboard, on a list to play in the tournament.

"I suck at beer pong, Franny," I whined.

"You will be fine," she reassured. "Plus, think of it this way... free beer."

* * *

AFTER TWO GAMES of beer pong, I found myself in desperate need to sit down. It only took moments for Franny to find herself a new partner, and I relaxed on the sofa, looking on. She was in her element, landing the Ping-Pong ball in the opposing cup effortlessly. She had an audience cheering for her before the first game was complete.

"All done playing for the night?"

A voice jolted me back to reality, and I realized that a guy I had never met before was seated next to me. He looked like he stepped out of an Abercrombie & Fitch advertisement. It might have been the beer or maybe just pure attraction?

I sighed, trying desperately to keep my cool. "I have definitely hit my limit on drinks for one night," I explained, consciously aware that I was slurring my words.

"I hear ya," he agreed.

"What are you drinking?" I asked, nodding toward his water bottle that clearly did not contain water.

"Vodka sunrise," he replied. His eyes were wide with excitement.

"What's in that?" I laughed, steadily focusing my eyes on his like he was explaining the cure for cancer.

"Oh, it's just orange juice, vodka, and grenadine."

I smiled. "Then why not just say that?"

"Say what?" He laughed.

"Why don't you just call it what it is? Vodka, OJ, and grenadine?"

"I like the name vodka sunrise!" He moved closer to me on the couch. Our knees were touching. That, mixed with the alcohol I already consumed, left me feeling a little breathless. I decided that I liked this person.

"I suppose," I answered. "As long as I can try some?" I reached for his water bottle and took a sip of his drink. I handed it back to him. "Do you go here?" I asked, surprised by my boldness.

"Maybe," he teased.

I nodded my head and smiled. "I go here. I am graduating this spring," I said as I took the beverage from him and drank a little more.

He gave me a high five, a little harder than I expected. He laughed, and I realized that my new friend was also feeling his share of tipsy. "I'm graduating too," he said enthusiastically. "Business major." He handed me the bottle, and I took another sip. It burned on its way down, in a good kind of way.

"No way! I'm majoring in business too!" I shrieked.

"What are the odds?" he asked, moving closer to me once more as he spoke. "What are you going to do after graduation?"

"I plan on opening my own business..." I explained as the orange juice burned a bit on its way down.

"Badass," he replied.

* * *

ABOUT AN HOUR LATER, my head was spinning so fast that I couldn't even make out the faces around me. I remember holding his hand and walking away from Franny. I don't remember walking to the bedroom, but I do remember telling him how much I liked him. I remember him asking me if he could kiss me. I had nodded eagerly but wished in the same breath that the room would stop spinning. I really liked him, but I couldn't see his face clearly anymore, which was sad because I liked it.

The bedroom had two sets of bunk beds, and I laid down on the bottom bunk that was closest to me. I wanted to close my eyes, but I also wanted to kiss him. He climbed up on top of me and continued kissing me.

"I can't stay awake," I moaned, frustrated that the kissing

might have to stop soon. But he ignored my complaint and continued to kiss me, my face, my neck, and my chest.

"You're so beautiful," he said as he lay down next to me. I pulled him closer and inhaled. He smelt of sandalwood or cedarwood... not sure which, but he smelled perfect.

"Thanks," I mumbled. He took my breath away when he removed his shirt. I couldn't see straight, but in my mind, he was immaculate. I decided that this was a dream. He was a dream come true.

"I think I love you," I whispered.

"Do you now?" he asked in between breaths, kissing more of my body than I could keep track of. *When did I take my shirt off?* I asked myself.

"Mmhmmm," I agreed.

I remember kissing him. I remember pulling him on top of me. I don't remember much after that, but I remember enough to know that we had slept together. When I woke up the next morning, he was nowhere to be found. I didn't even know his name.

* * *

AT FIRST, I didn't tell anyone what had happened, not even Franny. It wasn't just that I slept with a guy I didn't know or the fact that he was only the second person I had ever slept with in my life. It was more the embarrassment of knowing I threw myself at him and threw up in his bathroom several times before completing a walk of shame back to my place. I silently hoped that he was so drunk he would forget me. Chances were I wouldn't be seeing him again anyhow.

It would have been easier to put the incident behind me if it were not for the fact that I was late—very late. Franny stood with me in the bathroom of our small apartment when

I took the test. I cried deeper sobs than I had cried in my entire life. She held me and told me it was going to be okay.

"This is a nightmare," I wailed.

"I know. I'm so sorry," she cried.

"What am I going to do?"

"I don't know," she whispered. "But we should probably start by finding the guy from the party. You know... the dad." She hesitated.

"No!" I cut her off. "We are not notifying him. We are not contacting him, ever." My words were sharper than I had expected them to be. But I didn't take them back. Something snapped inside of me, and in that moment, I became a different person. In one night, I managed to morph from a carefree college senior to, well, a mom. Survival mode kicked in, and I didn't want help. Especially from *him.*

She shook her head. "Hazel, this is serious," she pleaded. "I know Bastian, the president of the fraternity. We can find out who he is..."

"Promise me," I demanded. "Promise me you will leave this alone."

"Okay." She sighed. "I promise."

* * *

THE REST of senior year went by quickly. Thankfully, I didn't start to show until well after graduation. The morning of my graduation was spent over the toilet with morning sickness, and I was almost late to the ceremony. My parents, who flew down from Maine for the event, were so proud of me. It was quite the bubble to burst when I shared my news.

They begged me to come home. They pleaded with me. "You worked so hard for your career, Hazel," they cried. "Come home and let us help you."

That was the moment that something stirred inside of

me. Something so life-altering and game-changing that I knew I would never be the same. *They didn't think I could do it.*

"You don't think I can do it?" I snapped.

"It's not that we don't think you *can* do it, Hazel," my father argued.

"Then what?" I asked, one hand on my hip and the other on my belly.

"You have no idea what you are up against," my mother affirmed. "Parenting, it's hard enough when you are ready."

My face grew hot, and my hormones raged. "I'm going to do this myself," I insisted. "I don't need help." And I didn't look back.

CHAPTER SIX

*M*y heart raced in anticipation. Jason had been stopping by the cottage periodically over the past week or so. Our encounters had been short-lived but truly wonderful. He really was a gentleman, and although I was certainly old enough to take care of myself, he honored my father by asking him permission to take me out on a date. Our days together consisted of walking the shore of Long Sands Beach. I had grown to appreciate the way the cool water felt as it brushed up against my ankles while we walked, hand in hand, for what felt like miles.

Long Sands Beach was also where we shared our first kiss. We were seated on the shore, on the cool and soft sand, overlooking the ocean. It was high tide, and the waves had been enormous. We watched as surfers enjoyed riding one after another in the distance. I had rested my head on his shoulder, and he had kissed my forehead, like he'd done many times before. I'd reached up and touched the side of his face with my hand and lifted his sunglasses over his forehead.

"What are you doing?" he asked.

"Looking at you."

"Why look at me if you can kiss me?"

I was surprised by his boldness, and it shook something inside me. I placed my other hand behind his head and pulled him close. His lips met mine, and for a moment, we were the only ones in the universe. I pulled back and laughed when his mustache tickled me so badly that I couldn't stand it anymore, and he vowed to shave it off if it meant more kisses like that.

I flattened the last section of my hair with an iron. My mother hated when I used a clothing iron on my hair. She was certain I would burn down the house with it. I assured her I would unplug it when I was finished. I adjusted my bubble top and pulled up the waist of my bell-bottom jeans. Satisfied with the way my hair and makeup turned out, I rummaged through my suitcase until I found my brand-new Dr. Scholl's wooden sandals. I cursed them under my breath as I fastened them to my ankles, knowing that they would cause my feet nothing but agony, but I was still determined, as they made my outfit even more stellar.

"Emiline," my mother called from the living room. "Jason is here!"

Already? How had I missed him? I could usually hear the sound of his Bronze 1969 Dodge Charger pulling into the driveway, but somehow I missed it. "Coming!" I called. I sprayed my neck and wrists with my favorite perfume and touched up my lipstick. I grabbed my purse and a sweater and headed for my bedroom door. I made my way down the hallway and into the living room, where Jason stood with a bouquet of red roses. "Hey, Fancy Pants!" I called. It was a nickname that I had given him in effort to honor our first encounter.

"Hi, beautiful."

My mother's smile couldn't be any bigger if she tried. "Those are gorgeous!" she exclaimed.

"Hi," I said, as I took the flowers from him. "These are beautiful, thank you." He looked handsome in his jeans and tan sport coat. His black, wide-collared shirt revealed a dark patch of hair on his chest. I jumped back in surprise, as the man who stood before me bore a sudden change in his appearance. "Jason! You shaved your mustache!"

"I told you I would," he said. He winked, and I felt the heat rush through my body. He looked like himself but younger in a way. Although I missed the edginess it brought to his overall image, I wasn't sure how long I could wait before kissing him.

"I like it," I said. "Let me just put these in some water," I said, gesturing toward the flowers.

"Don't be silly, dear," my mother interrupted. "I'll take care of the flowers."

I nodded and thanked her for her kindness.

"Where's Dad?" I asked, looking around the room.

"He made friends downstairs," she explained. "He really likes it here. I'm not sure I will ever be able to get him to leave this place," she joked.

"Okay, then," I agreed. "Shall we?" I asked, nodding toward Jason.

He looked me up and down and smiled. "We shall."

\* \* \*

THE NIGHT WENT BY QUICKLY, almost too quickly. Our dinner was remarkable. Jason introduced me to his favorite Italian food. I had never really fancied Italian cuisine, but when he put a bite of his meatball on his fork and gently held it to my lips, I had no choice but to take a bite. The flavor and the texture of that meatball was like nothing else I had ever experienced. He insisted I eat his last one, and in that moment, I knew there was something special about him.

Dinner was followed by a few rounds of bowling and a walk on Short Sands Beach. We thought about calling it a night but decided to visit the piano bar where Jason worked. He ordered me a Tango, his favorite drink. It was absolutely scrumptious. After two Tangos, I had declared that the orange vodka combination was the most delicious concoction in the world. When it was time to drive me home, I put up quite the fuss. "I don't want the night to end," I whimpered. We sat in his parked car, overlooking the rocks of the Nubble. It was well past curfew, but the idea of my father waiting up for me was far out of my mind.

"Then let's stay here a while," he whispered.

I nodded and climbed into the back seat of his car. He followed my lead and did the same. I grabbed onto the wide collar of his shirt and pulled him close. My fingers traced over his chest. His skin felt warm against my touch. I lay down on the leather seat of his car and pulled him on top of me. Kissing him with the absence of his mustache was exhilarating. His skin felt smooth against mine. He placed an eager hand behind my head and pulled me closer. His hands felt warm, and his body seemed to surround my entire being.

"Emiline," he said between breaths.

I nodded, as if agreeing to something brilliant he just said. I helped him slide out of his sport coat. He tossed it in the front seat and continued kissing me. My hands moved under his shirt and reconnected around the small of his back. I pulled him tightly against me.

"Is this too fast?" he asked.

I shook my head no, but a voice in the back of my head warned me to slow down. The same voice began taunting me, asking me what I thought I was doing. In one week, I would be on a plane back to London, and Jason Davis would remain here, in the States. I begged the voice to go away, but it wouldn't subside. Jason reached under my tube top and began to pull it down. He kissed the crease of my neck and my collarbone. The heat from his lips circulated through my body at record speed. His mouth met mine once more and began to move toward my chest. His fingers worked quickly as they started to unbutton my jeans. The voices in my head grew louder and echoed in my mind like a guard dog in a fierce panic. I placed my hand on his and removed it from my waistline. "Wait," I whispered. "Yes, you're right, Jason. It's too fast. We should stop."

He adjusted my shirt back into place, covering my naked chest, and nodded. He rested his head in between my neck and chest. His heart was beating rapidly. "You're right," he agreed.

I could sense his frustration, and I felt bad, but I reminded myself that we would both feel worse if we slept together and I left for London in a week. What good would that be for anyone? I ran my fingers through his hair and closed my eyes. "I leave in a week," I whispered.

"I know," he said. "I don't want you to leave."

"I'm not sure I have a say in the matter," I confessed. A tear escaped from the corner of my eye. He kissed it away and pulled himself off of me. He turned on his side, and I did the same. We lay there in silence in the back seat of his car, facing each other in the darkness.

"Emiline?"

"Yes?"

"You're pretty far out." His voice was calm as he flattered me, but his eyes blew his cover. He wanted me as badly as I wanted him.

"You're pretty far out, too, Fancy Pants."

He wrapped his arms around me and pulled me close. I didn't think it was possible for him to hold me tighter. How could I be falling for this man so quickly? It had only been a week, for heaven's sake. I allowed him to hold me for what felt like hours. I could sense his melancholy through the pattern of his heartbeat and the few tears that trickled down his cheek that I tried my very best to ignore, realizing in that moment that I had gotten pretty used to keeping people out. It certainly was easier than letting them in.

CHAPTER SEVEN

*M*y head is pounding as I reach over and shut off the alarm on my cell. How could it already be morning? How late did we stay out last night? I glance at the time, which reads 5:45 a.m. I stretch my arms overhead and replay the events of last night over in my mind. I will need to research Russell Cooper online and see if my assumptions are true. Not that it matters either way. I will never let him find out about Ellie.

"Good morning, sunshine," I say as my sleepy ten-year-old wanders into my bedroom. She is still in her nightgown and is clenching her elephant. Her mess of blond hair brings new meaning to the term bed head.

"Hi, Mommy," she replies. She moves quickly to the empty side of the bed and climbs in with me.

"How did you sleep?" I ask.

"Okay," she says. She pulls the covers over her and snuggles next to me. "Can I stay home today?" she begs.

I squint my eyes and examine her. She doesn't look sick. I feel her head and cheeks, and she doesn't feel warm. "Why would you stay home?"

She peeks up at me with her dark eyes and shrugs. "I just don't want to go." She pulls the covers up over her face, and I retreat underneath them too. She giggles. "If I stay home from school and you stay home from work, then we can actually be together," she whispers.

My heart almost shatters at her words, and I pull her close. "I know we don't get to see each other often, and I am sorry about that," I say. "But you know I have to work, Ellie... and you need to go to school." My voice trails off, and I am distracted because she smells like strawberry shampoo. It does feel really nice to lay here with her. "We will have a special day soon," I promise.

* * *

I TAKE a sip of my coffee and try to focus on the screen in front of me. The spreadsheet is organized and accurately calculated. I wish I could say the same for my disarray of thoughts. I spin my chair around to the shelf behind my desk and reach for my Dooney & Bourke wallet. I chew lightly on my bottom lip as I study his business card. The night had ended awkwardly to say the least. Russ returned to his table after my rude dismissal and was most likely wondering how his drink of choice, vodka sunrise, could have been so offensive. We were barely in the Uber before Franny was all up in my business, demanding to know what just happened. When I told her that he wasn't my type, she had argued that he could double as Justin Hartley, and he in fact was one hundred percent my type, and he was *hot*. The emphasis she placed on the word hot did not go unnoticed.

I had bit my lip and sighed. "Justin Hartley is way cuter," I responded, not looking up from my phone.

My mind wanders back to this morning, to Ellie's confession regarding my absence. Part of me is thankful that she is eager to spend time with me while another side of me affirms that I am in fact doing the best that I can with the cards I was dealt. But it wasn't Ellie's fault I got knocked up senior year of college, leaving her without a father. She asks about him often, and each time, I am forced to recite the version of a story that Franny came up with that consisted of her father and I meeting on a Carnival Cruise senior year of college and losing touch, as he lived on the other side of the world. I realize that this story is absolutely ridiculous, especially because Franny and I never could have afforded a cruise back then, but I figured it was better than the truth: Mommy drank too much at a frat party during spring break and met Daddy and then *bam!* There you were... a tiny little vodka sunrise miracle.

I sigh and realize that I do need to make more of an effort to spend time with my daughter. I search through the calendar on my computer screen and figure out how to make it happen. After moving two event consultations from the afternoon to the late morning and assigning my assistant to a venue showing in my place, I start to log into the school dismissal change app to let them know that I will be picking Ellie up instead of Gabrielle. Just as I go to click submit, my phone lights up with an incoming call, a client for an upcoming child's birthday party. A twelve-year-old girl will be having the most glamorous spa sleepover for her thirteenth birthday. I answer the call and decide that I can handle dismissal procedures later.

* * *

I SHIFT gears and voice dial Gabrielle. My day has been a whirlwind, and I couldn't even find a second to eat lunch, let alone to remember to tell Gabrielle she doesn't need to pick up Ellie. I hesitate for a moment and almost hang up the phone, tempted to head straight home. Gabrielle can pick up Ellie, and I can be at home when they arrive. The idea is tempting, and as the exit approaches that would lead me home, I come close to putting my blinker on. Instead, I continue on. I've made it this far; I can't stop now. Gabby's cell goes to voicemail, which, for this time of day, is surprising as she is usually in her car on the way to the school. I dial again and leave a message. "Hi, Gabrielle! Listen, I've decided to pick up Ellie today and surprise her. She mentioned something to me this morning, and it isn't sitting right... anyways, you don't have to pick her up. In fact, why don't you take the night off tonight. Text me and let me know you got this. Thanks!" I exit the highway and grow eager with anticipation at the idea of surprising my daughter.

MOMENTS LATER, I am secure in my spot in the parent pickup line. In order to be at the front of the school for pickup time (which is roughly between 3:00 and 3:10), I need to be in line at 2:30. It is 2:35 as I pull my emergency brake and shift my transmission to neutral. I contemplate taking the top down and decide it is just too hot. I poke through the glove box and retrieve the pickup pass I received at the start of the school year. Each family is given two passes. The badge consists of a copy of my license, along with a QR code that is scanned at pickup. I have one, and Gabby has the other. I cringe as guilt washes over me, and I realize that here it is, late May, and I haven't needed this pass once. I shrug it off as I often do and scroll through the calendar on my phone, cross-referencing the timing of tomorrow's events with the notes my assistant, Sidone, sent over. Everything seems to be in order, so I check my voicemail messages and my texts. Again, nothing from Gabrielle. There is a voicemail from my mother, begging me once again to come home and spend some time with them. *Not in this lifetime*, I think. It's not that I don't love my parents. I love spending time with them, and there are times I wish that Ellie could be close with them. I just can't fathom the idea of packing up and heading home for the summer when it is one of my busiest times of the year.

The clock reads 3:00 p.m., and like clockwork, the line starts to move. The car in front of me is a black SUV, and the car behind me is a minivan. The colossal sizes of the two vehicles make my Mustang seem miniscule in comparison. The line moves slowly, but I am still so far back, and it seems to take ages before I am driving into the school parking lot. I pull up closer to the large concrete building. Palm trees flank the driveway to the building. Big yellow busses line up across the drive. Herds of students walk toward the buses while others walk toward the pickup line. Teachers with walkie-talkies encompass the entrance, scanning passes with their cell phones and communicating student names to their part-nering parent pickup volunteers by the stairs. Students are lined up behind orange cones, and for a moment, I am so impressed with the system that I almost miss my daughter squeezing past two children in front of her, moving toward a cone. *That's weird,* I think. I haven't scanned my pass yet, so how would they know Ellie is ready to go? Ellie has mentioned multiple times that Gabrielle picks her up at the same time each day, so maybe she just knows when to get into the line? I check again to make sure that it is Ellie, and I am sure of it. She has chosen to pair her favorite pink-and-green tie-dye shirt with her most comfortable pair of denim shorts. Her blond hair has always been one of my favorite features about her. But now that I have been reunited with Russell Cooper, I suddenly have mixed feelings as I study her. I shut down those thoughts quickly, a strategy I have picked up as a defense mechanism over the years.

It is finally my turn, and I pull up to the cones. As I do, a teacher approaches my car, and I roll down my window. The black SUV in front of me prevents seeing Ellie any longer. I can't wait to see her face when she realizes I am here. "Eleanor Lavigne," I state, handing her my badge.

"Ellie Lavigne?" the teacher asks.

"Yes. Ellie," I confirm.

She appears confused and shakes her head. "Ellie was just picked up," she explains. She crinkles her nose in confusion.

"What do you mean, just picked up?" I roll my eyes, annoyed that Gabby has ignored my voicemails and texts. "By the nanny?"

She shakes her head. "Hold on a second." She puts her finger up as if to say, "One minute," and begins asking questions into the walkie-talkie. The line has been stopped this entire time, and I can see the problem up ahead. A mother is struggling to fasten her kindergartner into the back of her car, and it has caused a standstill.

"I communicated through the app this morning," I start but stop. *No, I didn't*, I think. *I never hit submit in the stupid app.* "I'm sorry." I laugh. "This is a big miscommunication. I'm Ellie's mother, and I forgot to notify you." My voice trails off, and the line is starting to move again, cars creeping in what seems like slow motion ahead of me. I strain my neck, trying to see around the SUV so I can wave to Gabrielle and show her that I am here, but I still don't have a visual on her.

The teacher pokes her head in my window, looking more confused than ever. "The main office says that you did send an email this morning," she confirms.

"Um, no," I respond, annoyed. "I did not."

"We have email confirmation from you, Ms. Lavigne, stating that Ellie's father would be picking her up today."

My breath catches in my throat, and I straighten my shoulders back, the shock from her words apparent in the expression on my face. "Her father?" I start to ask, but I stop. "What car is she in?" I shout. The teacher tries to form words but is suddenly at a loss and points to a white SUV that is pulling out of the parking lot. I notice the blinker on the automobile signaling left. Part of me wants to scream while another part of me wants to cry. *What on Earth is going on?* I rub my hands over my face and try to breathe, but my heart is racing. The white SUV is departing from the parking lot, and it is in this moment that I morph into a version of myself that hasn't surfaced until now. Blame it on too much crime television or just plain Mama-bear instinct, but I snap. "Move!" I shriek. I shift my car into gear, thankful that the teacher is moving out of the way. I drive quickly, maneuvering around the other cars in the parking lot, take a left, and drive as fast as my car takes me until I am one car behind the white SUV. The windows are tinted, and I can't see much.

"Dial 911!" I shout at my car, my voice catching and breaking, almost not pronouncing the numbers clearly. There are times when my dreams turn into nightmares, and for whatever reason, I need to dial 911. Every single time it happens, I fail. My hands are either too shaky or my words can't find their way to the surface. I am thankful that at this moment none of that is really happening.

"Calling 911," the car complies.

The light turns green, and I continue following the SUV. My mind is racing and my stomach turning. The thought of Ellie inside a stranger's car is too much for my mind to comprehend.

"911, what is your emergency?"

I try to speak clearly, but it is like I parachuted into one of my dreams... my worst nightmare. "My daughter," I cry. "My daughter has been kidnapped."

I try to explain as quickly as I can everything that is

unfolding. From the miscommunication in the pickup line to the reality that Ellie is in the car with a stranger. A man, maybe? Someone pretending to be her father. I am thankful for the speed of my car as I am able to stay within a distance that allows me to read the license plate numbers to the woman on the other end of the line. She explains that they are sending help and asks me to continue talking to her. "What do you see now?" she asks. I give her the details once again of my location, tears streaming down my face and questions spinning through my head at hurricane speed.

I have only been chasing the SUV for about ten minutes, but it feels like years. In this time, I have been able to give the 911 operator information about Ellie: her name, date of birth, cell phone number, information about the tracker app on her phone, and what she was wearing the last time I saw her. *Saw her.* To think I was just sitting in my car, only feet away from my baby girl and now... now this. Now she is in the back seat of that car, and who knows what horrible things are taking place. I sob harder.

"When are they coming?" I shout more than ask.

"They are on their way," she answers. "You are doing an amazing job, Hazel. Let's stay calm."

"Help my baby!" I roar. "You need to stop them. Now!" Tears begin to blind my eyesight, and I am so overwhelmed by the unfamiliarity of my emotions that I think I might faint. But I can't faint because I need to find whoever did this and kill them. With my bare hands.

"Any minute now," she reassures. "Any idea who might be driving that SUV, Hazel?" she asks calmly. How can she be so calm?

"I do," I state, convinced more than ever that the timing of last night's events could in no way be a coincidence. I use my knee to hold my steering wheel steady and reach into my wallet. I keep my eyes on the road but glance down at the business card in my hand. "Russell Cooper," I state. "I have his contact number here. He is my daughter's father, and he showed up out of nowhere last night."

She thanks me for the information and continues to tell me how great I'm doing. She asks me about Ellie, and I tell her that she is the most beautiful and talented little girl that I know, and that she got the shit end of the stick when it comes to parents. I cry harder as I say these words and pray to God that if He keeps my Ellie safe that I would be a better mother.

"Okay, Hazel, the state troopers are approaching. They are going to attempt to pull him over."

"I see lights behind me!" I shriek.

"Good! Now what I want you to do is pull over to the side of the highway in a safe spot. An officer will meet you there."

"I can't pull over!" I argue. "I need to stay behind her."

"Hazel, it is for your safety."

I hate that she is right. "The police are going to get her back to me, right?" I plead. There are lights behind me, and I need to pull over. My heart breaks as I turn off my car and it rolls to a stop. My fists hurt from punching the dashboard. By the time the officer approaches my car, I am unbuckled and rummaging around for my purse, eager to get out. "My baby!" I wail. "Please, please, please…" My voice trails off.

\* \* \*

I HAD to leave my car on the highway and rode back to the station with a police officer named Officer Clark. I am seated in a chair next to his desk. I realize that I have never actually been inside a police station before. I have texted both Gabrielle and Franny. Gabrielle still has not returned any of my texts. Franny is on her way. Officer Clark places a bottle of water in front of me. I open it eagerly, the cool liquid soothing me. He had asked about Ellie's dad and his possible involvement on the ride over here. The name Russell Cooper did not come up when they ran the plates to the SUV, but they called him in for questioning regardless.

"The car was registered to a man named Charlie Brambrilla," he says now, seated at the desk across from me.

I throw my hands up in frustration. "I don't know who that is."

"I do," he says, shaking his head. "Ms. Lavigne, have you ever found yourself on the wrong end of owed debt?"

"Debt?" I ask. "Like didn't pay a parking ticket or something? Student loans?"

"No, like gambling debt?"

"Gambling? I don't even buy scratch tickets," I reply. "Why are you asking me this? What does it have to do with my daughter? Did they stop them yet? Are you still able to track her from her phone? I can't see her location anymore on my app."

"They haven't stopped him yet. But he's surrounded. Listen, the Brambrillas are bookies in the area. They don't mess around."

"Bookies?"

"Yes."

"But I don't gamble," I reaffirm.

He nods. "Sometimes with these kinds of things, especially with these guys, loved ones of those in debt can sometimes go missing." *Missing?* Was that the plan for my daughter? If I hadn't shown up to surprise Ellie, then would she have been sold to the highest bidder to pay off someone's debt? *What the...*

"Hazel!" We are interrupted by Franny, who is running toward me so fast I think she might knock both of us over. She is holding her favorite pair of black Jimmy Choo pumps in her hands as she runs, something she often does if she is in

49

a hurry. Her bare feet move quickly across the tile floor of the station.

Relief floods over me as she hugs me tighter than I have ever been hugged in my life. "Ellie!" I cry into her shoulder.

"We will find her," she promises. "Who do you think took her? How did this happen?"

I throw my hands to my face and cry. "I don't know. They are bringing her father in for questioning..." I start. Judging by the look on her face, I realize she has no idea what I am talking about.

"Last night at the bar." I sob. "The guy who bought us drinks..." My voice trails off, and I don't need to finish explaining.

"Why didn't you tell me that it was him?" she shrieks. She sits in the empty seat next to me.

"I didn't figure it out right away, and I wasn't sure. But now I am."

"But he isn't the one driving?"

"Officer Clark was just telling me that the man who took Ellie is a bookie," I state. I throw my hands up in the air as if to say, "Why not?"

Franny makes a face and pulls her pink hair up into a messy bun. She can't sit still to save her life on a good day, let alone in an emergency. "A bookie?"

I nod. "Yeah. Weird, right?"

"So, he takes bets?" she asks the officer.

He nods. "High rollers, mostly."

"Like in casinos?" she asks.

"Yes, for sporting events, mostly."

"I don't even like sports," I reiterate.

"You don't," she says slowly. "But Ellie's nanny does."

## IN THE PRESENT- RUSSELL

### CHAPTER EIGHT

*T*his started off just like any other day for me. It was actually looking to be a really good day. I didn't have to wait in line too long for my coffee at Starbucks this morning, and my intern handled two of my closings this afternoon, which left me with extra time to go hit some balls at the golf course. So, imagine my surprise when the state police showed up to bring me in for questioning right when we were about to tee off at the eighteenth hole. I never got to finish my game.

Now, as the officer begins questioning me, I know right away that this must be in regard to the Amber Alert I received right about the time we started our game. *Ten-year-old girl abducted from her school. White SUV. Blond hair, hazel eyes, wearing a pink-and-green shirt with blue jeans. Abducted at 3:10 p.m., Hollywood, Florida.*

"What could I possibly have to do with this?" I ask, going from concerned to annoyed. I wipe the sweat off of my forehead. The small room I am in for questioning is not air-conditioned, and for a moment, it starts to close in around me.

"Do you have children, Mr. Cooper?"

I chuckle. "Me? Kids? No."

"We have reason to believe that you are the child's father," the officer states, like he is confirming that there is a slight chance of rain in the forecast.

"Me? The father?" I laugh. They most definitely have me mixed up with someone else. "You've got the wrong guy," I affirm.

"You never had sexual relations with a woman named Hazel Lavigne?"

"Hazel?" I stop for a moment. "I think I had drinks last night with a woman named Hazel," I tell him. "But we didn't have relations, as you call them. But even if I did, that's a little quick to conceive, birth, and raise a ten-year-old girl." I scoff. "Can I go now?"

"Ms. Lavigne recognized you at the bar," he explains. "She said you first met at a frat house during her senior year of college. She wasn't sure it was you, so she didn't plan on reaching out. But when..."

"But when her daughter got kidnapped from school, she figured it could be me," I finish for him. I run my hands through my hair and close my eyes. Hazel hadn't looked familiar to me at all. But I did party at the Kappa Beta house a lot during my college days. And I did have a few one-night stands back in the day.

"Mr. Cooper?"

I frown, and suddenly, I can't look him in the eyes. "I can't promise you that I am not her father," I admit. "But I can guarantee you that I have nothing to do with this."

He nods, and for a moment, it looks like he believes me. "Mr. Cooper, are you a gambler?"

A gambler? I think for a moment. "I play blackjack," I confess. "Is that a crime now?"

"No," he says. "But the driver of the vehicle that has

abducted your alleged daughter is affiliated with the Brambrillas."

My eyes widen. "Brambrilla, like Charlie Brambrilla?" *Holy shit,* I think. This is bigger than I thought.

"The media doesn't know that yet." He puts his finger over his mouth as if to say, "This is top secret."

I nod. "I understand."

"It's all over the news," he says.

"I'm sure it is."

"The FBI is getting involved." He emphasized the FBI like this would somehow make me change my answers.

"Look," I said, "I have nothing to do with this," I promise. "Hazel, the girl's mother. Is she here? I would like to see her."

He laughed. "I'm afraid she isn't up for visitors, Romeo."

I don't know why I suddenly need to see her, but I do. The thought of leaving the police station and heading home to follow the story on the news is too much. What if she is my daughter? What if there is something I can do? "If I am the girl's father, then don't I have a right to be here?"

He studies me for a beat then nods his head. "Let me check in with Officer Clark and see if she is up for it."

SHE IS SITTING NEXT to the officer's desk with the other girl from last night, the one with the pink hair. Her head is on her friend's shoulder, and she is crying tears the size of golf balls. She is not the same girl from last night. The woman from that bar was put together, confident, and in control. The one sitting before me now appears fragile. Her brown hair is matted to her face as she cries. She repeats her daughter's—our daughter's?—name over and over again. *Ellie.* I can't help but wonder if I have a daughter named Ellie. The sudden realization is both joyful and devastating because if she is my daughter, then I am the father of a little girl who is victim to a kidnapping and involved with a police chase that is now on every news channel in the state. I'm not sure what is scarier, that or the idea of being a father.

"Hazel?" I somewhat whisper.

She looks up at me, her back straightens, and her shoulders hike up toward her ears. "Russell," she responds.

"It's just Russ," I correct, and I am immediately embarrassed for correcting her at this moment. "They questioned me, and I want you to know that I have nothing to do with this," I said. My hands are in my pockets, and I glance at the floor. "But...I..." I can't get the words out. How exactly does one start a conversation like this?

"I'm sorry you found out this way," she says, sniffling between words.

The other girl studies me for a moment. She stands up and gestures for me to sit down. "I have to use the ladies room. I'll give you two some time," she says. She stands and walks away barefoot. She looks more than eager to exit the current situation.

"You don't need to apologize," she responds. I notice that her bottom lip is quivering, and her knees are shaking.

"You really think she's mine?" I ask, surprised by my boldness.

"I know she is."

I think about putting my arm around her shoulders in an effort to comfort her, but it seems odd given we don't really know each other. Which is even weirder, seeing as though she is saying that we made a kid together. I study her face. I wish I could remember her, but I just don't. I inch closer to her and take her hand in mine. "They will get her back," I promise. I hope to God this is a promise I can keep.

# IN THE PRESENT- HAZEL

## CHAPTER NINE

*We* are glued to the news report, and I feel as though I might be sick. Franny is seated to my left, and Russ is to my right. Franny hasn't taken her eyes off of him. I know what she is thinking. Russell Cooper is the adult, male version of my ten-year-old girl. It's too much to process right now.

Nobody can get a hold of Gabrielle. She is not answering her texts or her voicemails. An officer is heading over to my house to see if she is there. I was also able to provide them with the make, model, and license plate of her car. I am worried something terrible has happened to her. How could I not check in on her when she hadn't answered my calls and texts?

"How long have you known your nanny?" the officer asks.

I think for a moment. "I hired her when Ellie was just about a year," I say. "Just about nine years ago, I hired her."

"And you have never had a problem with her before?"

"No!" I exclaim. "She's been... wonderful," I choke. "I just want to know that she is okay."

"I'm sure she is okay," Franny whispers. But I know just as

well as she does that she can't guarantee that either of them will be okay.

* * *

THE TEACHER from the parent pickup line has been questioned along with the principal of the school and the superintendent. Officer Clark printed out the email communication that the teacher in the parking lot had referred to. The emails were sent from my address, but they were not written by me. They began three weeks ago where I explain that Ellie's father is back in the picture, and she would be spending time with him. They continue to explain that he has my permission to pick Ellie up from school. The teacher said that he did have a pass with a photo ID on it. When asked what the man's name was, she could not remember.

"I didn't send these," I repeated for the third time.

"That is your email address, correct?" Officer Clark confirmed.

"Yes, but I didn't send them."

"Who else has access to your email account?"

"My assistant uses my email from time to time."

"This is more than just emails," he says. "Hazel, the person who wrote these emails… they know you enough to *be* you."

Franny and I make eye contact, and my heart sinks. There is only one person in my life connected enough to the school and Ellie to be able to pull this off. She knew how to be Ellie's mother because I had let her become just that. "Gabby?" I cry. I shake my head and bury my face in my hands. "Gabby? How could she?"

# IN THE PRESENT- ELLIE

## CHAPTER TEN

*T*oday in school we were practicing using the online thesaurus to find words that will spice up our stories. Now, as I sit in the second row of this ginormous car with a piece of tape over my mouth and my wrists tied together, I am busy creating a running list of synonyms for the word scared. *Terrified. Afraid.*

We are driving really fast. I don't recognize the man who is driving. I am immediately disappointed because this morning before dropping me off at school, Gabby had told me that she had great news. She said that my father was going to be picking me up. "I didn't know I even had a father," I had responded. She had insisted that Mommy was trying to surprise me. I talked to my teacher about it, and she confirmed that yes, my mom gave permission for him to pick me up, and he was picking me up *today*. That explains why the school guidance counselor upped my visits from a Lunch Bunch group that met once a month to an unexpected session earlier this week that got me out of a spelling test.

Gabby had explained that he would be in a big white car, and that he would have his pass with him. Something about the situation didn't feel right, but I trusted Gabby more than anyone else in the world.

It didn't take a genius to realize that neither of these men inside the car were my father. The one in the driver's seat had flashed his pass at the pickup spot, and Mrs. Campbell scanned it with her phone. She looked at him and then back at me with a quick "Have a great afternoon!" and walked away. Aside from the fact that one of them was tying my hands up before we even left the parking lot (I'm assuming a father would not do this), neither of them look anything like me. They both have dark hair and beards. The one driving has a voice that sounds deep and evil like a bad guy in a movie I once watched. I had nightmares for months after seeing it. I'm pretty sure if I survive this day, there will be more nightmares to come.

My hands are folded on my lap and are tied together with some kind of twist tie. They hurt. I rest my head on the window of the car and look outside. There are police cars everywhere. I look over my head and out the sunroof. There are helicopters flying above us. These are news helicopters. I know this because sometimes when we are in traffic from a car accident, there are helicopters like this. Gabby told me that if we are underneath one of those, then we could maybe end up on the news! Does this mean I am going to be on the news? The thought of this excites me a little bit, and then I think of Mommy. She must be so scared, and I wonder if she is watching the news.

I have so many questions. Why would Gabby lie to me? Where are they bringing me? My thoughts are interrupted because the car is making a dinging noise, and I know right away, based on the driver's reaction and the bad words he is yelling, that he is in fact running out of gas. Gabby and I ran out of gas once. We were on our way to watch the Dolphins play in Miami, and we had to call something called AAA, and they came and brought us gas. Is that what was going to happen now? The man is hitting his fist against the steering wheel. The man sitting next to me (the one who tied me up) leans forward, throws his hands up over his head and says more bad words. The driver has dialed a phone number and now has his cell phone up to his ear. My head starts to hurt, and I close my eyes.

"I'm running out of options, Franco!" he yells. The car is swerving back and forth. I open my eyes and study his face in the mirror. He doesn't look so scary anymore... instead, he looks a little bit worried. Between talking with his hands and holding onto his phone, he is doing a very bad job driving the car. "This was supposed to be an easy pickup," he scolds into his phone. "If I go down, you're going down with me."

"Call your guy," the man next to me says. "He is the one who got us into this."

My stomach rumbles. I realize that I haven't eaten anything since lunch. I wonder for a moment when I might be able to eat again. The thought of not knowing makes me even more scared, but it makes me angry too. Who do these guys think they are? I didn't do anything to them. What do they want with me? My heart starts to race, and my knees get weak like they do before a football game. I can hear the voice on the other end of the phone, and he sounds loud and scary too. "Change of plans," he says to the man next to me. "I'm pulling over in about a mile. They are sending another ride, but we have to get to the other side of the median. Grab her and go." *Grab her and go?* Do they think I can't hear them? Or do they think that just because I'm a kid I don't understand what's going on. *Nobody will be grabbing me,* I think. I listen as the man next to me raises his voice to the driver and starts rambling in a language I don't understand. Although I don't know the words, I can understand by his tone that he is not happy about this plan. I close my eyes and take a deep breath.

I peek through one of my eyes and study him. He is not small like I am. One of the reasons I am so fast is because of my size. He is large and muscular. He won't run fast.

I think about Mommy and how scared she must be. I think about this morning and feel sad that I tried to make her feel bad for having to work. My thoughts are interrupted once again because the driver is pulling off to the side of the road, and he is driving on the grass. The car ride becomes bumpy, and I scream, but it is muffled behind the tape that is over my mouth. The car spins around like I am on the teacup ride at Disney World. I am trying my hardest not to throw up, but it's hard. The man next to me is not buckled in like me, so his body is getting bumped around. *Good,* I think. *Now he will be slow and off-balance.*

The car stops fast, and I hear my seat belt unbuckle. The man next to me has opened his door and has me scooped up in his big hands. He is pulling me out his door. I start to panic, but I remember what my Mom told me once about boys. "If you ever need to get away from a boy, kick him in the..." My foot makes contact with the man's private parts, and he lets out a long and agonizing grunt and lets go of me. I fall onto the grass with a thud and spin from my back to my side and jump up. He tries to grab me again. I use my elbow to jab him in his side. The fat on his stomach bounces back at me. He seems to be taken off guard, so I run. I run as fast as I can back toward the road where police cars are lined up. I pretend that my hands are holding a football. A perfect complete pass thrown by my buddy Jamison. I sprint as fast as my legs can carry me, and I envision the end zone in front of me and fans cheering. I imagine people in the crowds yelling for me as I score six more points for my team. But there is no end zone. Just lines of police cars and loud voices. I open my eyes and see a police officer. He is running toward me, and others are running past us.

"Keep coming!" he shouts and waves me over. He is a superhero. I have never been so thankful for anyone. I am tired, but I run to him. I wish I could extend my hands up and grab him, but I can't. Instead, I keep running until there is nothing in front of me but him. He swoops me up effortlessly and carries me away from the scene. "You are safe now," he reassures. I try to respond, but my mouth is dry, and my head feels fuzzy. "Everything is okay now..." His voice trails off, and I only half hear what he says because I need to close my eyes now and go to sleep.

## IN THE PAST- EMILINE 1971

## CHAPTER ELEVEN

"*D*o you have any more luggage?" my mother called down the hallway.

"Just one suitcase," I called back.

"The car will be here to pick us up in an hour," she reminded me.

"Yes, I'll be ready."

I sighed and glanced around my tiny bedroom. Although I had only lived in this room for just a couple of short weeks, it very much felt like home. I sat on the edge of the twin bed and fiddled with the corner of the orange-and-brown afghan. The fuzzy fabric felt smooth underneath the tips of my fingers. I wanted to remember the smell of this bedroom forever. Although we traveled quite often, this was the first time I was able to experience the wonders of the sea in this way. This place would always hold a special place in my heart. Why, I fell in love twice here. First with the beach and second... well... a piece of my heart would always be with Jason Davis. I closed my eyes and thought about our nights together, the two of us curled up in the back of his Dodge Charger, looking up at the night sky. We had talked for hours, about our hopes and our dreams, our fears and our loves. And then we would kiss and hold each other for what only seemed like seconds but was well into the early hours of dawn, and each morning, I would hike up the stairs of the tall gray beach house, certain my father would have my head for missing curfew, but he never did. Maybe he sensed my happiness? Maybe my mother told him to lay off? Or most likely, he was anticipating the inevitable, the fact that this might just be the only time in my entire life I could possibly feel this joy. And the realization of this truth made the feeling of dread that formed in my stomach a reality.

I stood up and walked over to the window. My view of the sea from my bedroom was limited but enough. I traced my fingers over the white wicker rocking chair and picked up the navy-blue blanket. I hugged it to my chest and then pressed it to my face. I inhaled again, only this time remembering with fondness the night I met Jason Davis.

Oh, Jason. We had said our goodbyes the previous evening, and I asked him not to come say goodbye on our day of departure. Saying farewell to him and the Anderson Cottage in the same breath just seemed impossible. I carried the blanket out of the room with me along with my last suitcase. I would have to leave the blanket eventually, but for now, it was still mine—a part of me, just as this place would always be.

I wandered into the living room and smiled at my parents. They were seated at the table on the back porch, laughing with one another. They sipped their tea and smiled as they spoke. I had always admired their happiness; it just seemed so effortless. I had longed for a love like theirs, and for a brief moment, I got to experience it. My farewell to Jason had been filled with so many tears, so much sadness. I silently cursed myself for letting him in, letting him take a piece of my heart. But then again, I also wondered what was worse. To never experience the kind of love that my parents shared? Or to love so deeply and so fearlessly that you just simply needed them for your heart to keep beating… and then what? To lose that love?

I would surely miss this place. Breakfast at the kitchen table with my father. Tea in the afternoon in the quaint sitting room with my mother. Walks on the beach with Jason. Oh, Jason. My eyes filled with tears, and I hugged the blanket once more.

"Hello in there?" a voice called from outside.

"Hello?" I called. I wasn't expecting anyone at the moment, but certainly someone had just knocked on the storm door. I crossed the small kitchen and went to the door to see who was outside. I looked through the screen. "Is someone there?" I asked.

"Yes, sorry," a woman answered. "I knocked, but you didn't hear me."

I opened the door and stepped outside. A woman, possibly a bit older than me, stood on the porch. She wore white, high-waisted hot pants with a pink tank top. Her long red hair was pulled into a straight high pony. She pushed her sunglasses up over her eyes and rested them on her forehead. She extended her hand out to me for a handshake. "Hi, I'm Elizabeth," she said. "Elizabeth Chase." Her platform shoes allowed her to tower over me, and I felt miniscule in comparison.

"Hello." I wiped my eyes with the back of my hand, hopeful that my new acquaintance hadn't spotted my tears. "I'm Emiline. It's a pleasure to meet you."

"I was in town and figured I would check on the place for my dad," she explained. "He sort of takes care of the property at the Anderson Cottage."

"Oh, how lovely," I said, aware that I was still awkwardly

clutching the blanket to my chest. "Come in, please, do come in."

* * *

HALF AN HOUR LATER, Elizabeth and I sat with my parents on the porch sipping tea. You wouldn't have known it by the looks of it that we were ready to depart for London within minutes. However, Elizabeth served as the perfect distraction for my melancholy. I found her wonderfully easy to talk to. She explained that she was born in Maine but grew up in Boston. Her father, Joey Chase, managed the property with his friend Gerry, who was currently living out of the country. When Joey found out she was coming into town, he asked her to check in on us.

"How thoughtful," my father said. "Tell him everything was in tip-top condition."

"Yes," I agreed. "Everything was lovely."

"I'll be sure to let him know," she said. "This is definitely one of my favorite places to visit."

"This cottage," I started. "It's nothing short of perfect."

"Exceptional," my father added as he drank the last drop of tea from his cup.

"Yes," my mother agreed. "This is a special place; I am sure of that." She paused for a moment and tilted her head to the side as she spoke. "This isn't just a cottage. It's a home," she affirmed. "I can tell there are many happy memories here."

"I'll be sure to tell my parents," she said. "I'm pretty sure they will agree with you. Many memories here for sure." A soft smile appeared on her lips, and I wondered what juicy secrets caused Elizabeth's eyes to light up in that way.

* * *

WHAT SEEMED like a few short breaths later, I was making my way down the three flights of porch steps of the Anderson Cottage. I said farewell to my blue blanket along with my new friend, Elizabeth, and watched as she drove off in her yellow Super Beetle. It was quite possibly one of the cutest little cars I had ever seen. Just as her car pulled out, our ride to the airport pulled in. I had to look twice because as the car pulled into the driveway, Jason's Bronze Charger pulled in adjacent to it.

"Jason!" I cried. "What are you doing here?" My voice trailed off, and I shook my head. A lump formed in the back of my throat.

He hopped out of his car and closed the door quickly behind him. "I'm sorry," he explained as he ran a nervous hand through his shaggy brown hair. "Mr. and Mrs. Wilson, I just need a minute with Emiline."

"Of course," my father agreed. "Emiline, your mother and I will be in the car. Do hurry along. We don't have much time before we need to be in Boston." His words were calm and steady, but his eyes screamed, "Don't hurt my little girl, or I will hurt you."

"Thank you, sir," he answered quickly. He took my hand and pulled me over to the stairs. I took a seat next to him on the step, turned to him, and waited. I had so many questions for him. What was he doing here? Hadn't we already said goodbye? But I was at a loss for words.

"I'm sorry," he said, his words seeming to get caught in his throat.

"Don't be," I whispered. "I hate to leave you, you know." My voice broke, and tears ran down my cheeks. He wiped them away.

"Emiline, I think I'm in love with you."

A part of me wanted to scream, *how can you be in love with me? We just met?* But I knew the answer because I was pretty sure I was in love with him too. If this wasn't love, what was it? "I know," I said nodding. "I'm pretty sure I love you too." This made me cry even harder.

"Don't cry," he begged. "You will make me cry."

I laughed and wiped the tears off my face with the back of my hand. "So where does this leave us, then?" I asked, my eyes growing wide with curiosity. "I'm leaving... now... I'm leaving now," I repeated. I placed my head in between my knees and hugged them tightly. Surely, my heart was breaking into a million pieces.

He rubbed my back and then ran his fingers through my hair.

"Stop," I begged.

"Stop?"

I sat up and looked at him in desperation. "Yes, stop! This is torture. We said our goodbyes." I bit my bottom lip, my eyes not leaving his.

He nodded and reached into his pocket. "I want you to have this."

My shoulders straightened, and for a moment, the scene unfolded in slow motion. "A ring?" I gasped. "Jason, what are you doing?" My thoughts spun around my mind like a tornado. "Jason...I—"

"It's a friendship ring."

"A friendship ring? Like a promise ring?" I exhaled, and my shoulders relaxed. A slight laugh escaped from inside.

"Sure, like a promise ring." He chuckled. "You sure are far out, Emiline Wilson."

I nodded and blushed. He slipped the ring on my finger. It fit perfectly. The silver band was beautiful. Tiny, engraved stars lined the edges. "Jason, it's beautiful."

He pressed his lips to the ring and then kissed my cheek. "Every time I think of the stars in the night sky, I will think of you."

"That's beautiful," I whispered. The tears began again. "It's too much," I scolded. "You didn't need to go spending money on me."

"It was nothing," he affirmed. "It was actually my mother's ring."

"Does she know you gave it to me?" I gasped.

"She doesn't know yet," he answered honestly. "But she gave it to me a few years back and told me to give it to the girl I want to marry someday."

"You want to marry me… someday?"

"That depends. Would you marry me… someday?"

I wrapped my arms around his neck and squeezed him. I released him after only a beat or two and allowed my lips to meet his. The kiss was like a bonus prize, seeing as we had already shared our last. I pulled back and stared into his eyes, surprised to see he was crying too. "Jason Davis," I said. "Every time I look at this ring, I will remember your promise."

"I love you, Emiline."

"I love you too, Fancy Pants."

# IN THE PRESENT- HAZEL

## CHAPTER TWELVE

*M*y daughter's blond head is resting on my shoulder. Her JoJo Siwa headphones come equipped with a large cheer bow that fastens to the band, and it is jabbing into my neck. I'm not complaining. She hasn't left my side since the incident, and I don't blame her one bit.

"How much longer?" she asks. She is listening to music from her iPad, and her voice is louder than she realizes. Her legs are pulled into her chest on the seat of the airplane next to me.

I glance at my phone and pull her headphones off her ears. "About another twenty minutes," I whisper. She nods, removing her head from my shoulder, eager to see out the window of the plane. I play with the end of her french braid, allowing her tresses to intertwine in between my fingers.

It has only been a week since the kidnapping. At first, both Ellie and I couldn't seem to get enough sleep. She was checked in at the hospital and released that same day. We spent an entire twenty-four hours curled up in my king-sized bed. The two of us were so close that we only took up a tiny portion of the mattress. Franny had stayed with us for a few nights until we felt well enough to start getting back to normal, as Ellie called it. The truth is, there would be no getting back to normal for Ellie and me. Not in southern Florida anyways... at least for now. First of all, there was no escaping the reporters. Ellie thought about going back to school (she agreed that I could stay parked in my car in front of the building, but I was not allowed to park my butt on the school steps like I wanted to), but the reporters just wouldn't stay away. There were only two weeks left of school before summer vacation, so we made the decision for her to stay home.

It was even hard for me to get back to my normal routine. My assistant and the rest of my team agreed to take over for me so that our planned weddings and functions wouldn't be swarmed with media. Everyone wanted to know what happened. Why was little Eleanor kidnapped? But I was keeping my mouth shut. The investigation was still open, and anything I said could prevent me from getting the justice we deserved.

*Justice.* Can a person even find justice when something like this happens? When a person that you trust more than anyone else on the planet tries to sell your daughter to the highest bidder? What would I even say to her? "Gabrielle, how could you give away a child that you basically raised?" I cringe when I think of the influence I allowed her to have in Ellie's life, most of it positive but some of it... well... illegal, for starters. When questioned by the police, the kidnappers explained that it was Gabby who hacked the school's security system and Gabby who sent the fake emails. It turns out that Franny was correct; Gabby's love of sports was more than just for entertainment purposes. She placed bids, high bids on professional and college sports. And she was doing it right under our noses. Officer Clark called it aiding and abetting, which was a serious crime in the state of Florida.

How could she do something like this? Was she so in over her head with the bookie that the only way out for her was to help them kidnap my daughter? *Where are you, Gabby?* I think.

I squeeze my fists together and take a deep breath, something I have done many times this week. Why didn't she come to me for help? I would have gladly lent her the money or gone to the police. She had options. The men who kidnapped Ellie claim that Gabby copied her pickup pass and replaced her photo with the kidnapper's photo. They also told the police that she figured out how to make her own QR code, which allowed her to breach the school's security app. None of that mattered though because she was nowhere to be found. When Ellie, Franny, and I got home from the hospital, Gabrielle had vanished. Many of her possessions were missing from her bedroom, and the police were unable to locate her. Part of me hopes she's on the run, but another part of me, one that I don't recognize at all, won't be sad if she gets what she deserves.

I flinch and startle without meaning to, disgusted by my thoughts. Of course I want Gabby to be okay. She is just a kid. I think back to how I was in my twenties, and I realize that I, too, had made my share of mistakes. Getting knocked up at a frat house, for starters—not my finest moment. My thoughts skip away from the kidnapping, and I find myself thinking of Russell Cooper. He stayed with us until Ellie was safe. We had watched Ellie's escape on the news together. I had collapsed to the ground when the white SUV pulled off the road, and my daughter bolted from the car toward the police. I thought he might ask to come to the hospital. Part of me hoped he would. He decided not to and claimed that it would be a lot for Ellie. I was relieved because he was right in that regard. He gave me another one of his business cards. I gave him mine.

"I can see the city!" Ellie shrieks with delight.

I look over her shoulder, both of our faces pressed up to the small window. *Boston.* "I see it too!" I giggle, squeezing her in my arms.

"I wish we could spend a day in the city," she whines.

"I know, El," I say. "You know that Grammy and Papa are waiting for us back home." *Home.* How long has it been? I graduated high school and took off from Maine to Southern Florida that summer and hadn't looked back once.

"Are they picking us up from the airport?" she asks. Her brown eyes are wide with excitement.

"No," I remind her. "A car is picking us up at the airport and will drive us up to York."

"How long of a ride is it?" she asks.

"About an hour and a half," I answer. "Come on. Let's buckle up for our landing."

* * *

WHAT SEEMS like only moments later, we have retrieved our luggage and are approaching a man wearing a navy-blue suit and holding up a sign that reads *Lavigne.* Ellie is struggling to pull two of our suitcases, and I have two more, and although I know we can manage it ourselves, I am relieved to have a helper.

"Hi, I'm Hazel," I say to the man. I extend my hand toward his for a handshake.

"I'm Kurt. It's nice to meet you," he responds. "Hi there," he sings to Ellie. I find it funny how people talk to kids sometimes. *She's not a dog,* I think.

"Hi," Ellie whispers.

"Are these all your suitcases?" he asks.

"Mine and my mom's," she replies.

"You must be staying for a long time then!" he exclaims.

I cringe. "Must be!" I sing back, handing him a suitcase. The truth is, we have no idea how long we are staying. None of this has been thought through at all. It was Franny's advice to take my parents up on their offer. I knew she was right. Ellie needed a change of scenery even more than I did. Kurt takes Ellie's two suitcases, and I take my daughter by the hand.

"Looks like we are set to go," I say. Ellie is standing still with a serious expression. Suddenly, I realize that I haven't asked her if she needed to use the bathroom or wanted to get something to eat. I am so eager to get to our destination, I hadn't bothered to ask. "Ellie?" I ask again. "Ready to go?"

She shakes her head and turns serious. An unfamiliar look of worry washes over her face. She presses her upper lip firmly to her bottom and takes a breath before speaking. "Please don't take this the wrong way, Kurt," she states. "But I am going to need to see some ID before we can get in your car."

IT IS dark when we finally pull up to our hotel. Ellie, who had slept for the entire ride to York Beach, rubs her tired eyes and squints up at the sign. "The Onion Bluff Hotel?" she asks in confusion.

Kurt places our suitcases on the curb, and in the distance, I see my parents exiting the hotel and running up to us. "No." I laugh, helping her out of the car. "Read it again. It's the Union Bluff."

"Oh yeah." She chuckles.

"Look." I point. "Your grandparents!"

My mom looks like she hasn't aged a second since I last saw her. Her dark hair is shorter than it was the last time I saw her. But she looks great... happy. It is my father who seems to have changed the most. His hair is thinning with specks of gray. Salt and pepper, Franny would say.

"My baby!" My mom immediately bypasses me and scoops Ellie up in her arms.

I turn and greet my dad, and when I hug him, my knees feel weak, and it isn't until this moment when I realize how much I have missed them. The reality of the past week comes pouring out of me, and for a moment, I am a ten-year-old girl safe in her daddy's arms. The familiarity of his embrace provides an unexpected comfort. He pulls back and smiles at me. "Welcome home," he says.

"Papa!" Ellie wiggles out of my mother's restraint and jumps into my father's arms. Seeing my daughter with him makes my heart happy.

"Hi, Mom!" I say, greeting her with a hug.

"I've missed you so much."

I realize she is crying, and I look away so I don't cry too. "I know," I say. "I'm glad to be here."

"Let's get your stuff up to your room," my dad suggests.

"Good idea," I reply.

"Hazel," Mom says. "Are you sure you and Ellie can't stay at the house?"

And there it is. I knew this would happen upon our arrival. I had agreed to come home, but I wanted to do it on my own terms. Ellie and I would be staying in a beach rental. I just had to find one first. But for now, we would be starting our adventure at a hotel. Going to my hometown was one thing, but going to my childhood home was another. "Baby steps, Mom," I remind her. I take my last suitcase from Kurt, reach into my back pocket, and grab the twenty I have ready for his tip.

"I've got it," Dad insists, pulling out his wallet.

I hold my hand up as if to say, "No, you don't," and hand Kurt the twenty-dollar bill.

# IN THE PRESENT- HAZEL

## CHAPTER THIRTEEN

The hotel room is spacious and overlooks Short Sands Beach. The view is simply breathtaking. Ellie and I giggle together as we observe herds of dogs roaming free on the beach from the window. When I was younger, we had a dog named Oscar. We were allowed to take him down to the beach at the early hours of the morning. Some of my favorite memories with Oscar took place right there on this beach. His wet and sandy fur would stick to me as we rolled through the small waves of low tide.

"Look at that one!" Ellie shrieks. "He's so big, he looks like a bear!"

"You're right," I agree.

I had requested a room with two double beds, but Ellie insisted she sleep with me. I didn't mind at all. There were times I awoke during the night. I started suffering through nightmares and panic attacks as a result of the kidnapping, and they haven't gotten better... if anything, they have gotten worse. I reach for Ellie multiple times throughout my attempted sleep, so part of me is relieved she is right there with me.

I kiss her cheek and squeeze her tightly in my arms. "I'm going to get changed, and we can get some breakfast downstairs."

"Can I get my bathing suit on? So we can swim later?" she begs.

"Sure," I agree. I smile to myself, thinking of the Maine ocean in comparison to southern Florida. My little Floridian is in for a surprise.

"Thank you!" she replies. "I'll wear my two-piece and my new cover-up."

"Okay!" I respond, half listening because I am now scrolling through my texts and Facebook messages. I try hard not to read my emails, but it isn't easy. I can't help but want to check in with my assistant, Sidone, to make sure things are all right. It is almost painful thinking about all that could go wrong without me.

**Hazel:** How is everything going? Did you confirm with the vendors for the Martinez wedding?
**Sidone:** Yes! Everything is on track.
**Hazel:** Make sure you tell Franny what time to deliver the cake. I usually remind her.
**Sidone:** Got it!
**Hazel:** I'm not sure I mentioned it... but at the consultation, the bride was nervous about the weather. Reassure her that the inside of the venue is perfect for the photo ops she wanted. Then remind the photographer.
**Sidone:** Done!

I RUB the back of my shoulder with my hand and sigh. There is no way they will pull this off without me. I am the one who met with the bride, and I am the one who coordinated

vendors. Sure, we have contracts and notes, but my events—
especially weddings—*need* to be flawless.

"I'm ready!" my daughter's little voice calls from the doorway. She is leaning against the door to our hotel room,
sporting a hot-pink cover-up and matching flip-flops. Her
blond ponytail pokes out from behind her large black
sunglasses that rest on top of her head. Her beach bag hangs
over her shoulder, a shade of yellow so bright it matches her
smile.

"You sure are." I laugh, realizing that I haven't changed
yet.

"Let's go, Mommy! The beach is calling my name!"

I chuckle and realize that I haven't seen her smile like this
in weeks. I glance down at my phone. Sid is typing something back to me, and my first instinct is to sit down and
wait to see what she says. But the smile plastered on my
daughter's face gives me hope that things might just be okay,
and I toss my phone down onto the table next to me and
start getting changed into my own swimsuit.

HOURS LATER, we have purchased beach chairs, towels, and a
plethora of beach toys. Ellie is now the proud owner of a
plastic toy doll who surfs the waves of the ocean during low
tide. The Barbie-sized figure is a miniature version of my
daughter. She has spent the past thirty minutes placing the
doll in the water and chasing her back to shore. We are both
thankful for the distraction as the water is a bit too cold for
Ellie, as expected. I reassured her that it is still early in the
season, and it should warm up by late June. I had shuddered
at that remark, surprised that my subconscious was allowing
me to stay back home that long. The reminder prompted me
to quickly get on Vrbo and Airbnb, along with some of the

other rental property sites I came across while searching for houses the other day.

I pull up the cottage that has the highest rating first. A large four-bedroom house with a two-car garage in Cape Neddick by the Nubble Lighthouse. My heart warms, and I remember my childhood and the Nubble Lighthouse. My father taught me how to eat a lobster there, and by the time I was Ellie's age, I could put back a three pounder.

I close out of the window for that house. Although I am instantly craving lobster, I decide that Ellie and I don't need four bedrooms. Even if Franny were to come visit, we wouldn't need four bedrooms. Instead, I settle on a three-bedroom cottage right off of Seaberry Lane. Two bedrooms upstairs and one on the main level. A bathroom on each floor. Although this is small in comparison to our home down south, the idea of downsizing is somehow a relief, and as I click the appropriate buttons and enter my credit card information in the designated fields, a tiny voice in the back of my head whispers, "Welcome home, Hazel."

I place my phone back in my tote and glance up at my daughter. She is still skipping through the waves with her new toy. I lean back in my beach chair and close my eyes. I could drift off to sleep right here. The weather is unusually warm for Maine this time of year. The highs today will reach eighty degrees, which is almost unheard of for late May, early June. Ellie and I had giggled to each other at the sight of beachgoers in their swimsuits and braving the cold sea. I myself am not able to remove my long-sleeve cover-up, and I have draped my beach towel over my legs in an effort to warm up. I stretch my arms over my head and sigh, retrieving my phone from my bag once again. *I will stop checking it,* I lie to myself. *Just need to get past this one more event.*

I don't have any new text messages from Sidone, which is

a good thing. She has worked with me long enough to know my processes and procedures; I just hope she can pull through and make it as good as I could have. I glance up at Ellie again and see that she is now digging a hole in the wet sand with her hands. Water fills the hole that she is digging into the earth. As quickly as she digs, it fills back up just as swiftly. She turns to me and points at it, and I laugh. I quickly take a picture of her and begin to post it on Facebook, but I stop in my tracks. A feeling of dread forms in the pit of my stomach, and I clench my teeth together, tension forming in my jaw. This feeling is becoming all too familiar. I decide that I'm not ready to let the world know where Ellie and I are staying. Although the kidnappers are behind bars, we still don't know of Gabby's whereabouts. I hope she's okay. The fact that they are unable to locate even her car leaves lots of questions unanswered.

Instead of posting the picture, I scroll through my friend requests. I stop short and lose my breath, dropping my phone into the warm beach sand. "No freaking way," I mutter as I pick it up and attempt to clean it off. I do a double take of the name that comes up on my friend-request list. *Russell Cooper, no mutual friends.* I check on Ellie again and click on his profile picture. *Russell Cooper sent you a friend request. Lives in Dana Beach, Florida.* I click on his profile picture and pinch the screen of my device to zoom in and see him clearly, the reflection of the sun causing a glare that is beginning to hurt my eyes. Russell has chosen a photograph of himself on the golf course for his profile picture. He is wearing sunglasses in the photograph, so I can't see his eyes, but his smile is bigger than ever, and my knees grow weak when I recall once again that it is Ellie's smile. I click on the *About* tab and see that he has built quite the resume for himself.

**Works at:** *Owner and founder of Cooper Finances*

**Places Lived:** *Dana Beach, Florida. Lakeland, Florida. Fort Lauderdale, Florida*
**Contact Info:** *754-224-8137, cooper@cooperfinances.org*
**Relationship:** *Single*
**Basic Info:** *Birthdate: July 28, 1985*
**Schools:** *Florida International University*
**Check-Ins:** *Hollywood Beach Golf Club*
*Orange Brook Golf & Country Club*

I GLANCE up at Ellie again and notice that the hole she has dug for herself has turned into what looks like a small kiddie pool. I wave to her, and she waves back. I look back down at Russell's profile. *You're missing one thing on that profile, Mr. Cooper,* I think. *Father of Eleanor Francine Lavigne.* I hold my breath and click *Confirm. Request Accepted.*

# IN THE PRESENT- RUSSELL

## CHAPTER FOURTEEN

*J* sip the last drop from my glass and allow the ice cube to hit my teeth, the coldness causing an unexpected chill. I hadn't meant to drink that so quickly. It has been weeks since the kidnapping. I haven't been able to relax since. Before Hazel walked into my life (or walked back into it, I should say), I had a good thing going. I was doing what I loved to do, was going in the right direction with my career, and I had all the time in the world to myself. Now... well... now I can't even get a good night's sleep. I wake up at what seems like all hours of the night. And even when I am able to sleep, I dream of my alleged daughter. I hadn't actually met her, Ellie. But from what I can see on Facebook, she is, in fact, my kid. Her coloring, her smile... all of it. My sister, Felice, had agreed with me but also encouraged me to explore all of the avenues, even the ones I have pushed to the back of my mind. Just because she looks like me doesn't make her mine. I text Felice a screenshot of Ellie that I had taken off the internet. She agrees that yes, Ellie could possibly be my child, but there are other possibilities, and I should consider all of them. I know she's right. I asked her not to tell anyone, especially Mom and Dad. My older sibling is like a vault when it comes to keeping secrets. And a secret it would need to be... at least until I was able to sort through all of this. If only I could get out of my own way.

"Russell?"

I look up from my drink, blood rising to my cheeks in embarrassment. "Sorry," I manage. "Long day."

"I was like, where did you go?" Kelsey giggles. She pulls her long auburn hair off her neck and moves it to one side.

My eyes meet hers, and I'm suddenly embarrassed about my trance. "I'm right here." I laugh. I've never been good about hiding my feelings, and I can tell that my date can sense I'm struggling with being "present."

"Work stuff?" she asks.

"Yes," I lie. "Balls to the wall for sure."

"Me too," she agrees.

"How so?" I ask. I study her as she goes on about her day and her patients. I remember that she works as a dental hygienist. I see her mouth moving while she speaks to me, but her words are lost. I am somewhere else. I try hard to pay attention to her, but I fail miserably. Instead, I order another drink and do the best I can to look interested. I like Kelsey. After all, she's good people.

* * *

By the time we finish our dinner, and I am four drinks deep, I start to feel a bit better. The thoughts that once took over my mind seem a bit farther away now. Kelsey excuses herself for the restroom, and I use this time to check my text messages. It doesn't appear that anyone is looking for me. Anyone except my sister that is.

**Felice:** (45 minutes ago) How are you?

**Felice:** (32 minutes ago) Did she accept your friend request? Did you talk to her about it?
**Felice:** (25 minutes ago) Hot date tonight?
**Felice:** (10 minutes ago) Call me later. I need to know.

I ROLL my eyes and put my phone back into my pocket. My sister, always needing to be in the know. But I can't blame her for wanting to know more about my daughter. *Daughter.* I slide my phone into my back pocket. My heart beats faster, and my thoughts consume me once more.

"Want to get out of here?" Kelsey is back at our table. The warmth of her smile calms me in an unfamiliar way.

I signal to the waiter for the check, and soon, we are heading back to her place. For a moment, I feel like myself again.

IN THE PRESENT- HAZEL

CHAPTER FIFTEEN

*A*lthough it feels like days since our plane landed in Boston, it has been weeks. Ellie and I have settled into our cottage and have gotten into the groove of "beaching it," as Ellie likes to say. We have spent most of our afternoons together on Short Sands Beach. Ellie's favorite time of day is low tide. She enjoys digging in the cold, wet sand and playing with her new beach toys. We have also enjoyed evenings out with my parents. I have already consumed my share of Maine lobster, and my parents are over- the-moon excited to have us home.

I glance up from the book I am reading and check on Ellie, noticing that she has made a friend. Another little girl about her age is sharing her beach pails with her. They are digging in the sand together and laughing. *How long have I been reading?* I pull my phone out of my tote bag. 3:00 p.m. "Yikes," I say out loud. "Where did the time go?" I reach my arms over my head and inhale as the salt air flows into my lungs and relaxes my soul. I can't remember the last time I have felt this composed and carefree. I stretch my legs in front of me, and my toes burrow themselves farther into the sand. It feels cool against my feet.

I toss my book onto my beach chair and walk toward shore. Crowds have lessened since this morning, and now that the tide is out, the sand stretches as far as I can see, and there is more beach space than there was upon our arrival. The waterfront seems to span for miles, and I am surprised at how far Ellie has distanced herself from me in the process. I laugh out loud as I approach and see her tangled mass of blond hair on top of her head. She had insisted on wearing her hair down this morning. I make a mental note to pick up some detangler at the store before heading back to the cottage, as we were most definitely going to need it.

"Hi, Mom!" She waves.

"Hi, El," I reply. "How's it going?"

"Mom, this is my friend, Zoe." She smiles, and I don't think it's possible for my daughter to smile any bigger.

Zoe looks up from her pail and smiles back. She appears to be about the same age as Ellie, but it's hard to tell. She is taller than my daughter, but most kids in her grade are. Her dark hair is pulled up in a messy bun. I am immediately jealous that this tiny human's mother won the battle of the hairdo this morning and wouldn't be fighting a pile of rat's nests and tangles for hours on end like me.

"We are making ice cream sundaes out of the mud," Zoe explains.

"Very nice," I say. I watch as the two girls dig into the muck. They act as though they have known each other for years. Gabby used to say that Ellie was able to make friends with anyone, whether it was at the park, the beach, or one of their football outings. Ellie would be the first one to ask if she could play. My stomach turns as I think of Gabby. She is still missing. I was convinced at first that the entire event had been her doing, but what if she was also a victim? Either way,

I make a mental note to never trust anyone with my daughter ever again.

"Hi there!"

As a voice interrupts my thoughts, I turn and see a woman walking toward me. I smile and greet her, knowing by the way she watches the girls that this is, in fact, Zoe's mother. "Hi," she says, waving hello. "Kayla, Zoe's mum."

I smile in response. "Oh, hi!" I say. "Nice to meet you." I reach out to shake her hand. "I'm Ellie's mom," I say, gesturing toward the girls. They work diligently on their project. Neither of them look up or even saying anything but somehow communicate and collaborate in efforts to produce the perfect beach-sand sundae.

She tucks her purple water bottle underneath her arm and reaches for my hand in return. "Are you here on vacation?" she asks. She adjusts her cap that reads *Mom Life* and pulls the dark strands of her ponytail through the back.

*Something like that,* I think. "Yes and no," I begin. "I grew up here, but I moved down south after college. I'm back visiting with Ellie."

"Nice," she responds. "Where down south?"

"Florida," I reply. I watch as Ellie and Zoe grab their buckets and sprint toward the water. "Southern Florida. Outside of Fort Lauderdale."

"I love it down there!" she exclaims. "That explains your tans." She chuckles. "Zoe and I are white as ghosts until at least July," she adds, looking from me to the shore, where the girls are gathering ocean water for their project.

"Yeah," I say in an awkward tone. I hadn't thought of Ellie and I having tans, but as I glance around me, I can see what she means. "Got to love that Florida sun," I say. "How about you? Are you on vacation?"

"No," she responds. "We live here, in York. My husband grew up here. We met in college."

"Where did you go to college?" I smile at Ellie, who is now dumping a bucket of water over her head and giggling. Zoe does the same. I shake my head and laugh. I love seeing her so happy.

"I went to Colby."

I nod. "A lot of my friends from high school went there," I say, smiling.

"Mom, look!"

I glance over to see Ellie back from the water, her and Zoe presenting us with their creations.

"We made sundaes!" she shrieks.

"No," Zoe corrects. "We made *sandaes.*"

All four of us begin to laugh, and I inhale, suddenly very comfortable with our new friends. Ellie gestures to me, asking me in the indiscreet way she does as if to tell me she has a secret and needs to whisper it. Normally, I would tell her, "Out with it." There was no need to whisper, but in this moment, I realize I am actually enjoying this side of her, and a secret from this muddy-brown-eyed beach bum could actually be fun. "What is it?" I ask.

She cups her hands over her mouth and leans into me. Her cold and sandy fingers scratch against my cheek. "Can we get ice cream?"

"Now? Aren't you having fun?"

"Yes," she whispers. "But I really like Zoe, and if we get ice cream, then you and her mom can become friends, and then I will get to play with her again."

I nod, surprised that I, too, would like to hang with Kayla and Zoe again. "If it is okay with her mom," I say.

She turns to Kayla. "Can we get ice cream?" she pleads.

"Yes, of course. Let me just touch base with Zoe's dad." She removes her cell phone from her shorts pocket and shields her face with her hand. She texts quickly and waits for a response.

"Ellie, go rinse off in the water," I instruct. She places her "sandae" by my feet and challenges Zoe to a race. Ellie beats her by at least ten yards.

"She's fast," Kayla observes.

"Like lightning," I say, quieter than I mean to.

"I don't know why he isn't texting back," she huffs. She places her hand over her eyes and searches the coastline. "Oh wait, there he is! Lucas!" She smiles toward the shore and flags down a nearby jogger. He had caught my eye before because, well, he is easy on the eyes, as Franny would say. His jog turns to a fast-paced walk as he makes his way over to us, smiling, his reddish brown hair waving in the cool Maine breeze. I study his perfectly defined six-pack as I often do when a nice six-pack comes my way but stop short when I realize that this beach bod looks familiar, all too familiar. He approaches us, a bit out of breath, and steals a sip of Kayla's water before making eye contact with me.

"This is my husband, Lucas," she says. She rolls her eyes and places her hand to her forehead. "Oh my goodness, I'm so embarrassed. I never got your name!"

My breath catches in my throat, and my heart beats faster. Beads of sweat rapidly start making their way down my back. I pride myself on my poker face. It is necessary in my line of work when it comes to planning and negotiating. But not today. Today there is no poker face. Because standing before me is Lucas Walker. And Lucas Walker is a man that I have spent the better part of twenty years trying to forget.

"Hazel?" He stares at me as if he has seen a ghost, his poker face failing him in the moment as well.

"Yup." I nod. "In the flesh."

"Holy shit," he replies.

Kayla does a double take and looks me up and down. "*You're* Hazel?"

I bite down on my lower lip and smile. *Get it together, Hazel.* But my knees feel weak, and I wish that I could sit down. "Yeah," I respond in some kind of weird choke of a whisper. "I was... well... I was Lucas's... girlfriend... back in the day."

"Small world." He laughs nervously and hands the bottle of water back to his wife. "It's good to see you," he says. "You look great."

Kayla's eyes seem to shoot daggers at her husband. "Small world indeed." She laughs nervously. I watch her as she studies me and wish that I could dig a hole in the sand and hide. If she is trying to disguise her jealousy, she is doing a terrible job. She looks from me, to him, and then back to me again. Her shoulders stiffen, and her cheeks turn pink. "You weren't just his girlfriend," she says, her voice quiet but her tone sharp.

I jump back, startled a bit by this comment. "What do you mean?" I ask. But I know what she means.

"Hazel." She snickers. "You weren't just his girlfriend. You were *the* girlfriend."

## CHAPTER SIXTEEN

*J* fiddled with the binding of my school yearbook. The dark-blue covering felt cool against me. It was warm for late May. Earlier that day, we sat as a senior class for one of the last times. We baked underneath the beating sun for what seemed like hours, rehearsing for our graduation ceremony, which would take place the next day. My stomach turned a little. I enjoyed high school. Most of my life, I was prepared to hate it. But it was actually kind of great. I hadn't expected it to end so quickly, and although I knew the time would come, I didn't think it would hit me this hard, like a ton of bricks.

I walked over to a vacant bench that overlooked the Nubble Lighthouse and took a seat. The roughness of the bench scraped against the crease where my shorts met my bare legs. I hugged the book close to my chest, like I used to hug my favorite stuffed animal as a child. I inhaled, exhaled, and allowed the salt air to calm me. I had always taken great solace in this tiny piece of heaven. I stared out over the rocks, past the dark ocean water, and studied the lighthouse closer. We had come here as a class once, to Cape Neddick on a field trip for art last year. Our teacher had provided us with a canvas and a pencil and asked us to do our best to sketch the famous landmark. We later painted it in class, and I was shocked when mine turned out half-decent. I had given it to Lucas for his seventeenth birthday. This was our spot after all.

I heard a car door close, and assumed it was Lucas. I flipped open my cell phone and checked the time. The digital clock on the front read 4:35 p.m. "You're five minutes late," I joked without turning around. I could hear him snickering as he ran up behind me, tickling the sides of my waist. "Lucas!" I giggled.

He stopped tickling me and surrounded me in a bear hug and squeezed me, planting a kiss on the side of my cheek.

"Hey, babe." He walked around to the front of the bench and leaned down to meet my lips with his. His kiss was warm and familiar.

"Hey, you." I smiled and kissed him back.

He sat down next to me and wrapped his arm around my shoulder. "You brought your yearbook."

"Yeah," I started, staring out at the water. "Weird thing. I've had this boyfriend since freshman year, and for some reason, he refuses to sign my yearbook."

He nudged me playfully. "I'll sign it when I'm ready."

I turned toward him, and our eyes met. I studied him, my boyfriend, my world, my... everything. His eyes were blue, like the ocean water before us. His chestnut hair glistened in the sun. He had been hesitant to sign my yearbook, but I assumed it was because he needed to write the perfect thing, something we could look back to when we were old and married with lots of kids (as we had discussed often). But as I stared through his familiar eyes and into his soul, I realized that something bigger was going on with him.

I cleared my throat. "Why don't you want to sign my

yearbook?" I hadn't meant to sound so serious, but there was no denying that the feeling between us was just that.

His eyes turned from lively to melancholy, and for a moment, I swore the warm breeze that once provided so much comfort had turned cold. He stared out over the water and made the face he made when he was deep in thought. His words seemed lost, and he was quiet.

"It's fine," I reassured, nudging him in return. "It's crazy, isn't it?" I ask.

"What?" he answered, both of our gazes out to sea.

"Everything, Lucas. One minute, we have this whole world of school, classes, friends…"

"Us," he finished for me.

"Us," I repeated. "And after tomorrow, it won't exist anymore." I hold back my tears.

"And us?" he asked, turning toward me and studying what felt like my every thought, my every breath.

"What about us?" I asked, surprised. How did I miss this? I could usually see things coming from a mile away but not this time. I held my breath and stared at the water in the distance. The whitecaps of each wave seemed to dissolve into thin air as it crashed against the shore. I noticed how the water broke over each separate rock, sometimes out of unison and sometimes synchronized with each other. I wondered if the water could feel actual pain from the sharpness of the rocks as it crashed so forcefully. I hoped, for the sake of the wave, that it didn't know what was coming, and that it couldn't feel a thing. That way it wouldn't have to anticipate what was about to come, just as I was doing in that moment.

"What about us?" I repeated.

He took my hands in his. "You're leaving. You're going to college in Florida."

"So?" I respond. "You're going to college too."

"I'm staying in the state." He raised his eyebrows and rolled his eyes.

I let go of his hand and crossed my arms around my chest, still clutching onto my yearbook for what seemed like dear life. "It's only a plane ride away," I reminded him.

He shook his head. "I'm not going to be able to fly down to Florida every weekend."

I put my face in my hands and sighed in frustration. Why hadn't he mentioned this before? Why was this suddenly the end of the world? "What, so you don't want me to go?"

"It's not that I don't want you to go to school. I just don't understand why it needs to be in Florida." His voice grew louder, and his tone was accusatory "You got accepted into two schools in New England."

I threw my hands up in frustration. "So you don't want me to go," I affirmed. "Lucas, this isn't a surprise. I've been talking about Florida since..." My voice trailed off, and I shook my head. Of course, he knew that I was accepted to school down south, but judging by the look on his face, he had convinced himself that I wouldn't go. It was true. I had gotten accepted into the other two local schools I had applied to, and one of them was Lucas's school. And although the idea of going to college with him made me ecstatic in ways I could barely comprehend, I couldn't help but long for a little bit of independence... a little bit of freedom. I pulled my knees to my chest and hugged them close to me. "Look," I said. "I'm going to school in Florida... but that doesn't mean we can't try and make it work."

"Hazel." He rubbed his face with his hands and sighed out of frustration. "You know I love you, right?" He removed my yearbook from its restraint and put it on the bench next to us. He turned toward me and took my hands in his, just as he had done so many times over the years. The hands that placed corsages around my wrist before prom were the same ones that wiped the tears from my eyes when I came up short of a passing grade in geometry and needed to go to summer school. The ones that once held my face while he kissed my lips, the first time we made love, and were the same hands that were holding on to mine now for what seemed like dear life. His stare was dark, and he chewed on the side of his cheek. "I do love you."

"Then what's the problem?" I found myself begging. "Luke, we have the whole summer… we have been together for almost four years… that's like the equivalent to an old married couple in high school years," I pleaded. "We can make this work." I threw my arms around his neck and pulled him close to me, my tears starting to soak the collar of his T-shirt. "Lucas… you're the love of my life." My words were muffled into his shoulder, but there was no doubt in my mind that he heard them. I know this because his arms hugged me tighter, and his sobs shook my body. "I can't possibly ever love anyone else the way that I love you."

"You're the love of my life too," he whispered. "That's why I need you to stay here with me."

I pulled away and wiped my face. "I'm going," I insisted. "And I just don't see the big deal."

"The big deal?" His voice grew louder, and a few tourists started to stare. "If you go to Florida, you will be ripping my heart out of my chest," he cried. He jumped to his feet, but I stayed seated, paralyzed with fear that Lucas, my Lucas, was breaking up with me.

I wiped my nose on my arm and pointed a finger at him. "You're breaking up with me because I'm going away to school?"

"No, Hazel… not because…"

I couldn't help it. I was furious. I had given everything to this person. I trusted him more than I had ever trusted anyone else. I trusted him with my thoughts, my dreams, my fears... and now this. "You're overreacting," I accused. My hands were on my hips, and I glared up at him. "We have the whole summer," I repeated.

He placed his hands on my arms and pulled me close to him. The tourists had moved on, and the silence of the moment started to sting the deepest part of my soul. "You've made your choice?" he whispered. "Florida?"

I nodded. "I'm going to Florida," I repeated. "But why does it have to be Florida or us?"

He pulled back and sat back down on the bench. He reached for me and pulled me close to him. I leaned down, my arms around his shoulders and my forehead against his as his tears soaked the front of my shirt. "Because you're incredible, Hazel. You're going to go off and do great things, and you are going to move on. And I just won't be able to pick up the pieces."

"You don't know that, Luke."

He nodded. "I do."

I closed my eyes and breathed in. "This is complete bullshit."

"Then stay here," he demanded.

"I'm going," I told him. I looked him in the eyes and begged him with my stare. "Don't do this," I pleaded.

"Hazel, if you're going... it's done."

"Done?"

"Over, with us."

I pulled back from him and gasped out loud in frustration. I shook my head and stepped away. I tried to find more words, but they didn't come. I would relive that moment over and over in my mind for years to come. What if I had argued? What if I changed my mind? But I would never know. Because at that moment, I picked up my yearbook, turned from him, and ran. Loud, monstrous sobs escaped from inside of me. I ran up the hill and toward the parking lot and didn't look back.

## IN THE PRESENT- HAZEL

### CHAPTER SEVENTEEN

"*I* figured it was only a matter of time until you ran into him." My mother sips from her mug and shrugs.

I jump, startled, and coffee almost comes out my nose. "Wait what?" I choke on my drink and stare at her, wide-eyed. "You knew that he has been living here?"

"It's not a huge town, Hazel. You know that. Things get around." She places her coffee down on the table in front of her and tucks a short strand of her dark hair behind her ear.

Was she getting a kick out of this? "You could have told me." I rest my coffee mug on my lap and tap my fingers on the ceramic rim. "It was just... a surprise, that's all. The way it happened... his wife's reaction... it was just... awkward."

"I'm sure it was."

The two of us sit on her front porch, the view of Long Sands Beach first thing in the morning is breathtaking. It's low tide, and from where we are sitting, the sea appears still.

"What was awkward, Mommy?" Ellie asks. She has been sprawled out on a beach towel on the wooden porch floor but has recently hopped to her feet. She removes her headphones and places them down on the table next to me.

"Oh, nothing," I answer. "I was just telling Grammy that it's a little awkward being home after so long," I fib.

She nods and puts her headphones back on.

"Are you going to see him again?" Mom asks.

"Lucas?"

"Yes." She chuckles. "Lucas."

I place my coffee mug on the table next to hers, stretch my arms overhead, and sigh. "Well... considering Ellie and Zoe have hit it off, I don't think I have much of a choice."

She studies me for a moment, the way a mother often looks at her child. I can tell, without even making eye contact with her, that she is making sure that I'm okay. I know this because it is the same way I look at my Elle. "I'm fine, Mom," I say to reassure her before she has a chance to ask.

"You always are, Hazel," she remarks. "It's just that... well... it's no secret that Lucas broke your heart, and I'm willing to assume that he is a big part of why you never came home..." Her voice trails off.

"I'm fine," I repeat. "But thank you."

"Have you heard anything from the police?" she asks, her voice turning to a whisper.

I shake my head and sigh. "Nothing," I say. "I called yesterday to see if they found Gabby yet. No such luck."

She takes my hand in hers and kisses it softly. "I'm just glad to have you here... it's truly wonderful."

"It's wonderful to be here," I say. And as I study her smile and the love in her eyes, I am overwhelmed with gratitude for her, and I realize that I am in fact happy to be home.

* * *

"How much longer?" Ellie whines from the back seat.

"We've literally only been in the car for five minutes," I say.

"I know... but it stinks in here."

She isn't wrong. My rental car has a unique stench that neither my mother nor I have been able to remove, even with her best cleaning products. She pulled out all of her odor-absorbing tricks, but I have yet to see a difference. I concluded, earlier that day, that it is a mix between stale cigarette smoke and spilled milk. "Two minutes," I promise her. "Are you excited?" I ask.

"Duh!" She giggles. "Of course I'm psyched. Zoe is awesome," she says, like I should have already known this information. "Did you know she is a year younger than me?"

"I didn't know that," I say. I turn the wheel of the rental and park in the parking lot for Short Sands Beach. Kayla will be meeting us here with Zoe. I say a silent prayer that Lucas will stay home. Our encounter on the beach was about a week ago, and I am only now beginning to shake it off. Since then, Ellie and I have met up with Kayla and Zoe, and so far, it has been smooth sailing. There are awkward moments where I feel like Kayla is studying me intensely, but I tell myself it could just be my imagination.

"Watch the cars," I instruct as we climb out of the black GMC Terrain and close the doors behind us.

"I'm so excited!" she shrieks. Her blond locks are pulled into low-braided pigtails underneath a bright-pink baseball cap. It slides around her head as she skips to the curb. Her boogie board drags along the pavement behind her. I resist the urge to tell her to hold it correctly, but the truth is that it's great to see her this happy, and I decide to pick my battles and let it go.

"There you are!" Kayla calls to us from the beach. It is high tide, which doesn't allot for much space to sit on the beach, but Kayla has claimed our spot and is busy spraying Zoe with sunblock.

"Hey!" I call, relieved that I don't see any sign of Lucas. Kayla has swapped her usual athletic one-piece bathing suit for a red bikini top and matching sarong. We approach Kayla and Zoe, and I place my chair in the sand. I rummage through my beach tote and find Ellie's sunblock. She has removed her cover-up and has assumed a sunblocking position before I have to ask. "How's it going?" I ask Kayla.

She rubs the last of the sunblock on her daughter's face and smiles. "Great!"

"High tide today," I note.

Kayla stands and adjusts her sarong. I hadn't noticed her defined abs before or how long her legs are prior to this moment. I silently curse my imagination because it is off and running. A movie is playing in my mind: I picture Lucas on top of her, cupping her face with his hands, kissing her the way he used to kiss me. And even worse, his lips sliding over her bare abdomen, moaning with satisfaction and telling her over and over again how beautiful she is—because that is what he used to say to me. *Dammit, Hazel*, I scold. *Get a grip.*

"Did you pack lunch?" she asks, sliding into her beach chair, her voice bursting the imaginary thought bubble over my head.

I finish sunblocking Ellie, and off she goes, hand in hand with Zoe. "Yes, I did," I respond. I open my chair and secure it in the sand next to Kayla. I grab my phone and my water and settle in.

"Zoe is so sick of peanut butter, but I didn't have time to go to the store, so that's what we have."

I smile and think of my mom this morning in her kitchen, making chicken salad from scratch so Ellie and I would have a nice lunch on the beach today. An unexpected and unfamiliar wave of relief and gratitude rushes over me.

"So," she starts, "don't be mad."

"Oh, gosh." I laugh. "Whenever something starts with 'don't be mad,' I get a little worried," I say. I watch Ellie and Zoe with their boogie boards. The waves are bigger than normal, and they are crushing them.

" So… Lucas and I were talking…"

I spin my head toward her so fast I think I might snap my neck. "About what?" I ask, failing to hide that I'm surprised.

"We have this friend… and it could be fun… I mean, if you could get out." She is rambling and floundering, and for a moment, I almost feel bad for her… almost. Because the long and short of it is that Lucas and Kayla want me to go on a double date. "So, what do you think?" she asks. She tips her sunglasses, and I can see a glimmer of hope in her eyes. Of course she wants to set me up. I'm her husband's ex-girlfriend. I'm much safer and less of a threat in her eyes if I'm not single.

"Oh, I don't know," I say. "Things have been complicated… and Ellie… it's just not the best time."

"You don't have to marry him." She laughs. "Warren Green is superhot. My girlfriends have described him as a mix between Jesse Williams and Laz Alonso," she says, her eyes wide. *Did she just lick her lips?* I think to myself. "Just come out with us. He is super nice too. It could be fun."

*Fun? I would rather get a root canal.* I sip my water and close my eyes, images of Lucas and Kayla not forgotten. I think back to the friend request on my phone from Russell Cooper and remember the trauma from the kidnapping, and for a moment, I am eager to let loose and have some fun. I am also intrigued by the idea of meeting this Warren Green. I have always had a soft spot for Jesse Willams. "When are you thinking?" I ask, surprising myself.

She squeals with delight. "Tomorrow night," she explains.

"We are going to hang at the piano bar and get some dinner and drinks."

I know exactly which piano bar she is referring to, and nostalgia rushes over me like the waves that are sweeping over my daughter's little blond, bobbing head. Lucas and I shared many special nights at the piano bar. I wonder if Kayla knows this. "Who is watching Zoe when you go out?" I ask, changing the subject in my mind.

"OMG, I have the best nanny." She claps. "Maybe she can watch both girls."

"I'll ask my parents," I say. "I've had really bad luck in the nanny department."

# IN THE PRESENT- LUCAS

## CHAPTER EIGHTEEN

*I*'ve always been the kind of guy that keeps a bucket list. You know, a list of the things that a person wants to do before they die. I've knocked a few of them off already in my short thirty-two years on planet Earth. Skydiving… check. Hawaiian honeymoon… check. I can state with confidence, though, an item that isn't on my bucket list: double date with wife and ex-girlfriend. Totally *not* on my bucket list.

Of course, Kayla spun the idea as if it were both of ours. To be honest, I only agreed because I could tell it would make her feel better. Since we ran into Hazel on the beach last week, there has been nothing except talk about Hazel and questions regarding how long we dated and more inquiries about whether or not I have been in touch with her since high school. I'm pretty sure Zoe got an earful over dinner that night. "She wasn't *just* your girlfriend," she repeated over and over again. "You loved her a lot… you told me as much."

I rolled my eyes and cursed myself for disclosing this to Kayla. It was true that I ended my relationship with Hazel, but it was Hazel who chose to leave. "And you're my *wife*," I had reassured her, reaching across the table and taking her hands in mine. "You have nothing to worry about... it was *so* long ago."

The truth is Kayla really does have nothing to worry about. Hazel and I broke up right at the end of senior year, and we literally haven't been in touch since. I met Kayla during my sophomore year of college. We were assigned to work together on a project, so we met at a coffee shop on campus. Coffee turned into lunch, and lunch turned into dinner... and well... the rest is history. Of course, seeing Hazel again has opened up a can of worms that I hadn't been faced with since our breakup. It was a rough breakup for sure. We were together way longer than most high school kids date for. That made it really hard. I also can't help it that she looks good. She looks like she could be in magazines for crying out loud, and she pulls it off without even trying. I almost wish she had gained a hundred pounds and wasn't attractive because maybe that would help Kayla cope with her return. But that just isn't the case. Florida life must suit her because she looks really good. Really... really... good.

And now, we are seated at a table in the piano bar, sipping cocktails and eating steamers. Kayla is seated to my right, and Hazel is directly across from me. My friend and colleague Warren is seated next to her. Warren and Hazel seem to be hitting it off, but it's hard to see clearly. The thick fog of awkwardness prevents me from making an objective observation about the situation.

We finish up our appetizers and order dinner and another round of drinks. Kayla orders wine, and Hazel orders a french martini. I don't remember her liking martinis, but then again, we were in high school when we dated. So truthfully, I really know nothing about her.

"What is it that you said you do for a living?" Hazel asks

Warren. I can tell by the way she phrases her question and the way she sits up straight with her shoulders back, drink in hand, that she is no rookie in the dating department.

"I'm a teacher," Warren responds. "I work at the high school with Lucas."

Hazel turns to me. "You work at the high school?" she asks. "Our high school?" Her cheeks turn pink when she says "our high school," but I pretend not to notice.

I nod my head in agreement. "Yes, ma'am," I answer. "It's like I never left."

"What do you teach?" she asks.

"American Literature," I respond, taking a sip of my drink.

"Hazel, tell Warren about Ellie!" Kayla exclaims. "Her daughter is the cutest."

"Oh, Ellie?" Hazel asks. "Ellie is my daughter. She's ten."

"Awesome," Warren replies. "Can I see a pic?"

"Sure," Hazel says as she rummages through her purse. I recognize her purse as a "mom bag," as Kayla likes to say. She calls it a purse, but it's really a bag. It completely blows my mind that my high school girlfriend is a mom. She pulls out her phone and swipes the screen open. She pauses, and a look of uncertainty washes over her. It's been a long time but not long enough where I can't read her. She focuses a moment on whatever it was that she read, the creases in her forehead revealing concern, and then eventually pulls up a picture of her daughter. "This is her," she says. "She plays flag football, see."

Warren admires the photo of Ellie and tells her that girls playing football are badass. She seems to like his comment because she relaxes a little, and they continue their small talk. Kayla nudges my knee with hers and makes her excited face. Her eyes are screaming, "It's going well." I smile and nod and sip my drink, hoping that hanging out with Hazel Lavigne isn't something we need to make a habit of. It's just so... I don't know, weird. I dated her in another life. We know absolutely nothing about each other. So then why am I jealous of the way she is looking at Warren? Or the way Warren is looking at her?

* * *

LATER THAT EVENING, we are on our fourth round of cocktails and are stuffed from dinner and desserts. A teenager who seems to be here with a group of friends is singing at the piano bar a classic version of "Piano Man." I smile as Hazel sings along with the words, and for a moment, I am a teenager again. Kayla has her arm wrapped through mine, and I can tell by the way she focuses on Hazel that she has her own insecurities she is fighting.

"Who are you texting?" Kayla asks Hazel.

"Just checking on Ellie," she replies. But her cheeks are pink, and I have a feeling she isn't being completely honest.

"How is she doing?" Kayla asks, a look of concern washing over her.

"Good," she replies. She turns back toward Warren and continues a conversation with him. I don't know if it is too many martinis or if she really thinks he is funny, but she is laughing hysterically over his dumb jokes. Nobody likes Warren's dumb jokes, especially the ladies.

I start to wonder about her. Who is Hazel Lavigne these days? What's her story? Who is Ellie's father? If Ellie is a year older than Zoe, then that means Hazel was pregnant before graduating college. I wonder how Mr. and Mrs. Lavigne took that news. I rub the back of my neck with one hand and take a sip of my drink with the other. Hazel pulls her long brown hair over one side of her shoulder and smiles at Warren, a smile that should be saved for someone she has known for years. She was always like that, Hazel. She would make friends wherever we went. So why does it surprise me now? *I have so many questions for you Hazel*, I think. *But somehow, I don't think I want to know the answers.* I sip my drink and smile, doing my best to play my role in the love story that seems to be unfolding before my very eyes.

## CHAPTER NINETEEN

*W*arren is smoking hot. I have to admit, I was hesitant about tagging along with Lucas and Kayla on a double date. I wasn't worried about the blind date aspect of the situation. I had been more afraid that being close in proximity to Lucas Walker for more than twenty minutes might make me spontaneously combust... or at least make my knees weak enough for him to sense my fear. But it turns out Kayla and Lucas have excellent taste in friends. I've gone on my share of dates over the years, and I can tell right off the bat that Warren Green is one of the good ones. Not only does he teach business classes at the high school (my favorite subject in school), but he also owns a business on the side. It is a nonprofit organization that raises money for local animal rescue shelters. Although I don't make it a point to spend my time running anything that has a "non" in front of the profit, I do have a weakness for a hot, handsome (and successful) man who loves dogs.

We have been deep in conversation for at least an hour, and I am enjoying his company. I'm not sure if it's the drinks or not, but Warren is very easy on the eyes. His dark skin looks smooth to touch, and his brown eyes strike me as mysterious and intriguing. His white-collared shirt sticks tight around his arms, and I find my mind wondering what it might be like to remove his shirt off his body. I quickly place my martini glass to the side and ask the waiter for water. Inappropriate fantasies about Warren will need to wait until I'm not seated across from my ex.

I excuse myself for the lady's room. Kayla and Lucas are in deep conversation and don't seem to notice as I make my escape. I flip through my Facebook Messenger before closing the bathroom door behind me. I lean up against the wall and read the messages that have been popping up on my lock screen for the past hour or so. Messages from Russell Cooper, Ellie's father.

**Russell Cooper:** I'm heading out of town for a bit, but I wanted to check in.

**Russell Cooper:** I've been looking at pictures of Ellie. You're right. She looks like me. So crazy. Not crazy in a bad way, obviously… it just blows my mind.

**Russell Cooper:** Sorry, I'm rambling. It's just that… I would love to hang out when I get back into town, but there are some things we should clear up first. I need to talk to you about the night… you know… the night we met. Maybe we could meet for drinks? Or talk on the phone? Maybe I could eventually meet Ellie? No pressure. Just let me know. Sorry for the awkward messages.

I SIGH and lean my head against the cool concrete wall of the single-person bathroom. There is a knock on the door, and I ignore it. My heart is beating quickly, and I grow dizzy. I make a mental note to drink more water upon my return to our table. I reread his messages and wince, knowing that now he can tell I've read them, one of the things I find most annoying about Messenger. Although I don't want to type anything, I know that it will look like I'm ghosting him. I close out of Facebook and open my texts. I have a missed one from my mom, letting me know that Ellie is tucked in nice and cozy in my old room and is already asleep. I also have many messages from Franny, creeping on my date. She wants to know what he looks like and if he is hot. She repeatedly asks how it's going. I smile and shake my head, thankful for my best friend.

**HAZEL:** Yes, very hot. And very sweet. Going great.

I CAN SEE that Franny is typing back to me, and I await her response. There is more knocking at the bathroom door. "Just a minute!" I call out.

**Franny:** Nice! What's his name? I'll look him up.
**Hazel:** LOL. Not giving you his name. You're such a stalker. Listen… Russell keeps messaging me. He wants to meet Ellie. I don't know what to say.
**Franny:** Russell? Ellie's dad? (Surprised face emoji)
**Hazel:** Yes.
**Franny:** Do you want him to meet her?
**Hazel:** I don't know what I want. I kind of want it all to go away.

I SEND a screenshot of his messages to Franny. In a quick moment, she begins typing back.

**Franny:** I don't know, Hazel. I mean, you haven't even done a paternity test.
**Hazel:** Franny, Ellie has his FACE. Besides, he was the only one I slept with since Luke.
**Franny:** I know. Just take it slow.
**Hazel:** ok.

I SWIPE out the text and enter Facebook Messenger where Russell's messages await me.

**Hazel:** Sounds good.
**Hazel:** Message me when you get back into town, no rush.

I TOSS my phone back into my purse and exit the bathroom. A line of three or four women are lined up. None of them are happy with me. I give them my best "sorry" face and continue by. A hand on my shoulder startles me. I turn in surprise, startled by the unexpected gesture, and see Lucas. He takes my hand in his and pulls me around the corner, away from our table where Kayla and Warren are seated.

"Lucas, what the hell?" I ask.

He takes my hand and guides me past the bar and out a door that leads to a stairwell. I am completely and utterly freaked out. His hands are sweaty, and I can see that he has had too much to drink.

"What are you doing?" The tone in my voice reveals my displeasure.

He places his hand on my shoulder, and I lean back against the cool concrete wall, realizing that I, too, have had too much to drink.

"I just need to talk to you... alone."

I study his eyes. They are the same eyes I remember, but in a way, they are not. "Now?" I ask. "You set me up with your friend, whom I really like, by the way, and now you need to talk to me?"

"I didn't set you up," he says, making his frustration clear. "Kayla did."

"Your wife," I say, placing emphasis on wife.

He nods. "It's just," he starts, "seeing you again... it's all just so surreal."

I cross my arms over my chest and frown. "Yeah," I say, rolling my eyes. "It's a real trip. Can we go back to the table now?"

"Who is Ellie's dad?" He cringes. "When did you meet him? Do you... did you... love him? Like you loved me?"

I remove his arm from my shoulder. "That's actually none of your business."

"I know," he says. He rubs his face with his hands. "It's just you were a big part of my life."

I nod in agreement. "You were a big part of mine too," I say. "Like a million years ago."

He runs his hand through his shaggy hair and sighs. "I'm sorry. Clearly, I've had too much to drink."

"Clearly," I whisper. "Lucas, we need to keep the past in the past," I say. I place a comforting hand on his shoulder. "We need to let it go."

"You loved me though?" I can't tell if he is asking me or

telling me.

"I did."

He is quiet and looks into my eyes. For a moment, I am seventeen again, a high school senior, standing there with my yearbook, begging him not to break up with me.

"I loved you," he confesses.

"I know," I whisper, my voice choking back tears. "But it's over... it's been over. It's time to let it go."

He smiles and brushes a strand of my hair behind my ear, something I remember him doing often. "Sometimes I wonder what would have happened if you didn't leave."

"You can't think that way." I realize that I am speaking to him like I speak to Ellie when she is being ridiculous. And he is, in fact, being ridiculous. "If I didn't go to Florida, I wouldn't have my business. I wouldn't have Ellie. You wouldn't have Zoe and Kayla."

His eyes grow wide, and he sighs, bracing the wall for support. "I know," he agrees. "And I love them."

I smile. "Of course you do," I say. "They love you, very much. Can I get back to my date now?" I joke. I wonder how long we have been gone, and I immediately begin to make up a lie in my mind about checking in on Ellie.

"Yes," he says. "But you need to know that it isn't easy for me, Hazel. You are one tough woman to forget." He leans forward and closes his eyes, clearly coming in for a kiss. I hold my hand up and stop him, inches from my face.

"Go back to your wife," I whisper, surprised at how strong my willpower is. "We are just friends now, Luke."

"Friends," he repeats.

"Friends." I pull him close to me and hold him for a beat, this man I once loved. I could hold him for longer, but he isn't mine anymore, and I let go of him quickly. "Go," I say. "I'll be five minutes behind you."

He leaves me there, in the stairwell, and doesn't look

back. Although my heart is flooded with sadness, it is also overwhelmed with relief. Because now, after all these years, I am able to let go of Lucas Walker.

I wait a few moments and head back to the table where I am comforted by Warren and his incredibly charming smile and his ridiculously large biceps. Warren and Kayla don't ask about my disappearance. I slide back into the seat next to him and sigh with relief as he wraps his arm around me.

"You're back," he says with a smile.

"Yup," I say in return. I glance up at Lucas, who is drinking a water that Kayla must have ordered for him.

Warren takes his hand in mine and smiles again. For a moment, the thought of leaving here with him sounds quite lovely. Lovely enough that I am even able to stop thinking about Russell Cooper and, quite possibly, my ex-boyfriend Lucas.

* * *

"Do you need a ride home?" Warren asks.

We are standing outside of the piano bar. Lucas and Kayla already said goodbye for the evening, and I was relieved when Lucas was no longer in my presence. "Oh, I walked here," I explain. "I'm right over on Seaberry Lane."

"Oh, okay, then," he replies. There is a moment of awkward silence between us. "Up for a short walk on the beach?" he asks.

Part of me is exhausted from our night out... probably more so from being around Lucas and Kayla. But the other part of me is curious about Warren. My new football-playing, business-teaching, animal-rescuing, hot-bodied friend. Plus, I'm not thrilled about going home to my vacant beach cottage. I haven't been away from Ellie since the kidnapping, and a piece of me feels empty without her. "I think a walk would be nice," I say.

"Okay, then," he says, his smile revealing excitement that is undeniable.

"You're really excited for a walk," I joke. We cross the street and remove our shoes.

"See, that's where you're wrong." He chuckles. "I'm not excited about the walk. I am excited about who I'm walking with."

I laugh and smile back at him, tucking my shoes underneath my arm. The sand feels cool and smooth against my bare feet. "I'm excited about you too." My face grows pink, and I silently curse the martinis.

He chuckles again and motions to my shoes. "Let me carry those for you," he insists.

"I can carry my shoes," I say, continuing to walk to shore. The tide is out, but it looks as though it is slowly creeping in. I am no stranger to Short Sands Beach in the evening. Most of my major events in high school—prom, homecoming—ended here on this beach in the darkness of the night.

He stops walking and meets my stare, the seriousness of his gaze taking me by surprise. "Hazel?" he asks with a soft smile. "You don't let other people help you often, do you?"

I roll my eyes and think about this for a beat. "I'm just saying that I can carry my shoes. They are, after all, my shoes."

He shakes his head and places a warm hand on my shoulder. "I'm not saying that you can't. I'm saying that I would like to. If you would let me."

I hand over my shoes, and he takes them from me. His hands are large, and he is able to handle both of our shoes in his grip. He takes my hand with his free one. We walk along the shoreline, allowing the chilly ocean water to poke at our toes as the tide creeps closer. The sky is clear, and I can see stars that I can't usually see back home. Being so close to the city makes it hard to see the night sky clearly. I inhale the familiar scent of the New England coast. There really is nothing like it.

"So, you grew up here?" His voice is deep and gravelly, and I like it.

"Yup," I answer. "You?"

"No, I actually grew up in New Hampshire."

"What brought you up this way?"

"They had a position open at the high school back in 2011, and I came up here to interview. Haven't looked back."

"Do you like teaching?"

"I love it. Especially teaching business."

"Well, there is a lot to know about running a business." I pause for a moment and cringe, thinking of Events by Hazel. I haven't checked in with Sidone all week.

"You're thinking about work," he accuses.

"Yeah." I laugh. "I am."

"Lucas was telling me that you run your own company. He was bragging about you."

"Lucas was bragging about me?"

"Oh, Lucas told me everything." He pretends to punch my shoulder and laughs.

"That was a long time ago."

"You messed him up pretty good," he says.

I rolled my eyes. "Lucas and I… that was another life."

"And that it was," he agrees. "Were you married?" he asks.

I stop short, startled by his question. He stops walking but does not let go of my hand. "Married to Lucas?"

"No." He laughs nervously. "I just know you have a daughter." His voice trails off.

"No… I've never been married."

"I'm sorry. I shouldn't have… that's personal."

I release my hand from his and rub my arms with my

hands. "Ellie's dad... it was a one-night thing," I explain, suddenly embarrassed. "I had too much to drink, way too much."

"That's cool," he says. "No judgment here."

I smile. "Thanks."

We continue walking.

"Is Ellie short for something?"

I nod. "Yes, it is short for Eleanor."

He pauses for a moment and tilts his head to the side. "I like Eleanor."

"Me too," I agree. "When I was pregnant with Ellie, I went through this metamorphosis, I guess you could say. My parents challenged the idea that I would be okay raising her by myself. It really hit a nerve. I wanted my daughter to be strong, so I needed a strong name. I had remembered an essay that I wrote on Eleanor Roosevelt. I was so inspired by her... by the way she led unapologetically, even though women back then didn't have the rights we have now. I want my Ellie to be strong like that. I *need* to be strong like that." I stop in my tracks, surprised at how easy it is to talk to Warren. Is it the drinks? Or is it just Warren?

He places our shoes on the lumpy beach sand and sits down. He gestures for me to sit next to him. I do, thankful that I chose my favorite pair of jeans and not the short black cocktail dress that I had originally intended to wear. He wraps his arm around me and pulls me close. I lay my head on his shoulder, thankful for this moment and thankful for him. The smell of his cologne is intoxicating.

"I think," he says, pausing to kiss the top of my head, "I think you are strong."

"Thanks," I whisper. *Kiss me again*, I think to myself.

"You know," he says, "just because you rely on other people for help, doesn't make you weak."

I stare at him for a moment. "I know," I agree. But do I

know? I have spent an entire decade trying to prove that I actually don't need help, that I can do it on my own. So much so, that I kept my daughter's existence hidden from her father. I kept her away from my parents, her grandparents. I trusted her with a stranger. She was kidnapped, for crying out loud. Who have I become? An event-planning, business-owning, self-absorbed monster, that's who. A tear escapes from the corner of my eye, and I wipe it away.

"Are you all right?" he asks. "I didn't mean to upset you."

I shake my head. "No, it's okay," I lie. "It's just... I don't know... I guess I feel like if I let people in, I'm setting myself up to be hurt."

He reaches up and traces the side of my face with his fingers. My face feels small and vulnerable against the magnitude and powerful feeling of them. "I think," he whispers, "that you might want to start letting people in."

"I know," I agree. I look up at the sky and admire the stars. The night is so clear that I can actually see them twinkle. "It's beautiful here," I say.

"I think you are beautiful," he says, not missing a beat. He leans forward, and our lips meet. I hesitate for a moment, immediately wanting to pull away, afraid of what this could or couldn't mean. But I don't pull back. Instead, I lean into him and reach one hand behind his head and the other behind his back. I pull him close to me and kiss him back. I allow myself to collapse into his kiss, to be lost in his embrace. I listen for the voice inside my head that usually warns me about the possibility of the inevitable heartache this could eventually bring, but it is absent in the magic of the passion we share.

I pull back and search his eyes with mine. I am lost for words. "Whoa," I manage to mutter.

He lies down on the soft, cool sand and pulls me on top of him in another embrace. "Whoa is right." He laughs.

I am overwhelmed by the feelings that run through me. I'm both excited and terrified at the same time. I decide that I need to kiss him again, and I do. He sits up, and I wrap my legs around his torso. He feels sturdy beneath me. I pull back, and we are both breathing heavy. "We should probably..." I start. *Take this inside*, I think.

"I know," he says between breaths. "We should stop."

I nod, knowing he is right but unable to avoid the disappointment that washes over me. "Can we do this again sometime?" I ask, a small laugh escaping from me.

He kisses me again, and my insides grow weak. "We better," he says. "I like you, Hazel Lavigne."

# IN THE PAST- EMILINE 1972

## CHAPTER TWENTY

Out of all the days and all of my life's finest moments, this one, by far, was the greatest. The day was picturesque, to say the least. The gardens at the Arundel Castle in West Sussex, England, did not disappoint. I will never forget the flowers, oh, the flowers in all of their elegance. They danced in the breeze as they surrounded us. A massive sea of purple, yellow, and white, with specks of red throughout. The tiny formations of colors were the sea, and Jason and I were a tiny island, a small speck of earth amidst an entire ocean of colorful blossoms. Just the two of us, hand in hand, underneath the bluest of blue skies, vowing to love one another forever and ever, husband and wife.

And then, all was quiet. The dancing had ceased, guests departed, and we were alone. The honeymoon suite was entirely ours. Mr. and Mrs. Jason Davis. I climbed into the gigantic bed that was ours for the evening. I pulled the sheets up over my shoulders and snuggled up against him. "Sleeping already?" I whispered.

He turned to face me, his eyes opening wide. "I'm awake," he says, a slight startle in his voice.

I place my finger over his mouth. "It's okay," I say. "It's late. This was quite the day. You should rest."

I traced his face with my fingers, and he gently returned them to his lips. He kissed them softly.

"This day," he said between kisses, "was the absolute best day of my life."

"Mine too." The darkness in the bedroom covered his face, and I moved closer to him. "I need to see you," I whispered.

He moved his face closer to mine, and I smiled.

"You're a very handsome man, Fancy Pants."

He kissed me, and I melted into him, just as I always did. I pulled back after a moment and studied him once more. "Are you really okay, with moving to London and all?"

"Yes," he said, kissing me again. "I'm really okay."

"Okay," I said. "I just want to make sure it's what you really want."

"It is," he said. "Now will you please kiss your husband?"

"Yes, sir." I laughed. "I just... I know that my father said..." My voice trailed off. Upon the announcement of our engagement, my parents bombarded us with questions. Where would we live? Would we stay in London? Move back to the States? Prior to getting engaged, I had taken a position at the local elementary school. They needed a substitute teacher, as the art teacher took maternity leave. I fell in love with it immediately and decided to return to school in hopes to someday be an art teacher. My father had implied that Jason could tend bar anywhere, and I could tell by his reaction he was not so impressed by my father's tone. His voice said congratulations, welcome to the family! But the look in his eyes and the judgment in his voice screamed, "You just aren't good enough for my little girl."

I pulled back from his kiss and rested my head on his chest. "I just want you to be happy," I whispered.

"I'm happy," he said, making the best effort to reassure me. "I'm happy that I'm with you."

"I'm happy that you're happy," I said. "With whatever it is you decide to do."

"That's what I love about you, Em," he whispered. "Now kiss your husband."

I smiled and pulled myself on top of him. The covers fell off my shoulders, revealing the white lace of my nightgown. He wrapped my legs around his waist and pulled me close, gently moving the strap down off my shoulder and replacing it with his kiss. My lips met his chest and kissed him as I traced my fingers along his abdomen and back up to his face. "Jason," I whispered, without even meaning to say a word.

"Emiline," he whispered back. "I want you... I want all of you."

I smiled, a small sense of satisfaction washing over me. The choice to wait until our wedding night was more mine than his, and I was not sure I would have been able to wait if it wasn't for our lack of alone time. He had only come to London one time to visit me since our initial meeting in Maine, and that was the trip he proposed. Most of our relationship, and our engagement for that matter, consisted of letters and phone calls. I needed a part-time job simply to cover the cost of my end of the long-distance bill. But in the thick of written communication and phone conversations, there was no denying the spark between us.

Jason lifted my nightgown over my head and tossed it to the side. In a mess of tangled kisses and somewhat clumsy undressing, my husband, in the darkness, lay above me. I couldn't see him, his body just a shadow that towered over me. But our souls connected in a way neither of us had ever known, and I knew in that moment that Jason Davis, my husband, was without a doubt a piece of me, and I would never let him go.

# IN THE PRESENT- ELLIE

## CHAPTER TWENTY-ONE

*I*t's almost July. As far as I know, we still don't know where Gabby is. And although I love being in Maine and spending so much time with my mom, grammy, and papa, I can't but help but miss life back home... especially Gabby. I have a hard time believing that she would hurt me on purpose, and lately, I have been so worried about her. What if the men who took me took her too? I feel bad talking to Mom about it. She seems so happy here. Just as I had made a new friend, so has she. His name is Warren... and he makes her smile... a lot.

I see a huge wave coming my way and turn to face my boogie board toward shore. "Zoe!" I yell. "Zoe, catch this one!" I turn to my friend and see that she is running through the water toward the wave.

"Got it!" she yells back.

We wait for the absolute best moment, and we both dive onto our boogie boards, allowing the tall wave to carry us toward shore. Cool ocean water sprays around me, and I am on top of the world. The wave drops us off on the shore, and we run over to where our parents are watching. Zoe's mom and dad are smiling and waving at us. My mom is sharing a beach blanket with her new friend, Warren. They are holding hands. Ew.

"That looked like fun!" Mom yells.

"It was!" I say, careful to avoid looking at their hands. It's weird to see Mom holding hands with someone. She only usually holds my hand. I've often wondered what it would be like to hold Jamison's hand. I blush at the thought of this and ask for a snack. My mom hands Zoe and me each a bottle of water and snack-sized portions of Goldfish crackers. Zoe and I take the snacks over to our towels, far enough to give my mother her privacy. *Seriously, Mom,* I think. *Stop drooling over Warren.*

"I think they like each other," Zoe whispers, as if reading my mind.

I squeeze some ocean water out of my ponytail with my free hand. "Ya think?" I ask sarcastically. "She hasn't stopped staring at him."

Zoe smiles. "My dad has been friends with him forever," she acknowledges. "He's really nice."

I roll my eyes. "I'm not saying he isn't nice. I just don't usually see my mom drooling over a guy. It's just... different."

"Well," she says. "What does she usually do?"

"What do you mean?" I ask. I wipe some Goldfish crumbs off my hand and onto my towel.

"For fun? Back home?" she asks.

I think for a moment. "She just... I don't know... worked," I say.

"Not a bad thing, then," Zoe says thoughtfully. "Back home, she was working, and now she is here with you," she says.

"Yeah," I say. "Me and Warren."

"Come on!" Zoe shouts. "We are missing the waves."

"I'll race you to the water!" I yell.

"No fair!" Zoe argues. "You win every time!"

* * *

LATER THAT DAY, I asked Mom if we can have some time alone, her and I. She suggested we go for ice cream over by a lighthouse she used to spend time at when she was younger, the Nubble Lighthouse. I said, "Of course!" because I never turned down ice cream. Plus, I have some things I need to get to the bottom of with Mom.

The lighthouse isn't as big as I expected, but I do see what she loves about it. It looks like it should be in a picture, and as we shopped around the gift shop prior to getting our ice cream, I noticed that it was in fact, in pictures, many pictures for that matter. Mom and I purchased sun hats at the gift shop because we forgot to bring ours from home. "The sun gets pretty hot here in July," she explained.

I had ordered my favorite ice cream, chocolate peanut butter with extra sprinkles. Mom ordered a vanilla soft serve in a cone. We walked as we ate our delicious treats and struggled to lick up the melting parts before it dripped on our hands. We talked about the new friends we had made here and how blue the sky looked. It isn't until now, as Mom is wiping up my sticky hands with a wet wipe, that we take a seat on the rocks overlooking the lighthouse and begin to really talk. Like really, really talk.

"Do you miss your friends back home?" she asks.

I was quiet for a beat. "I miss football," I say. "And... I miss Gabby."

Mom is quiet, and I hope she isn't mad. She takes her hand in mine and meets my stare. "I miss her too, sweetie," she says.

I rummage through my small backpack and retrieve my glasses, placing them on my face, and turn back toward the lighthouse to study it. It's really pretty how it's on its own tiny mountain, with water surrounding most of it. I bet a lot of things have happened here over the years. It feels like this would be the kind of place where special things happen. Like magic moments. "I hope she's okay," I say.

"I hope so too," Mom says.

"I like it here," I say.

"You do?"

"Yes, I do. I really like Zoe and her family."

"I do too," she says.

"Zoe says that you and her dad were boyfriend and girl-friend," I say, holding my breath in anticipation of her response.

"Yup." Mom laughs. "We sure were, a long time ago. Actually, we used to sit right here," she says, pointing to the spot we were seated.

"And kiss?" I shriek. "Gross!"

"It wasn't gross," Mom says, laughing.

"It is gross." I laugh. "Kissing is gross."

"Someday you will understand," she says gently.

I nod, blushing, thinking of Jamison. "Are you kissing Warren?"

"Ellie!" Mom gasps. "No… I'm not kissing Warren."

"Yet." I chuckle. "You aren't kissing him yet. You are so in love with him."

"Eleanor Francine, I am not in love with Warren."

"Yeah, okay, Mom." Her face is red. I don't think she is mad, but it's hard to tell. "You must have kissed my dad though," I blurt. "Enough to make me."

It gets quiet very quickly. So quiet that I can now hear the sound of the waves crashing against the rocks, and I couldn't hear that before. I can hear voices of other people around us, and in the emptiness of the moment, I wish I hadn't said that. On one hand, I don't like to make mom uncomfortable by bringing up my father, but on the other hand, he is my father, and I deserve to know about him. I watch the way Zoe's dad plays with her, and I get angry, really angry. If I can't have a father, then don't I at least deserve to know about him?

"Ellie…" My mom's voice trails off.

"It's okay," I say. "You don't have to talk about him."

She places her arm around my shoulder and pulls me close to her. She smells good. Like ice cream and sunblock. "No, you're right. I did kiss your father," she admits.

I turn to her, surprised by any mention of my dad. "On the cruise?" I ask.

She shakes her head. "No, Ellie. Your dad and I didn't meet on a cruise," she confesses.

"You didn't?"

"No, we didn't," she says. "I met your dad at a party." Now her cheeks are turning pink, and this moment is awkward, and I really wish I didn't bring it up.

"It's okay, Mom. We don't have to talk about it."

She stares straight ahead at the lighthouse and doesn't seem to hear me. "I kissed your dad a lot that night," she says. "It was the only time I ever kissed him."

I nod, somewhat understanding what she means. I learned about babies and how they are made during health class when the nurse was giving the puberty talk. She was talking about our bodies and how they were changing, and one of the boys in my class blurted something about body parts and making babies. I was completely mortified and asked Gabby about it. She told me how babies are made, and now, as I sit here listening to my mother talk about it, I think I actually might throw up all of my ice cream.

"So, I didn't tell your father about you," she explains, "because we only kissed that once."

"And you made a baby," I blurt. "Me."

"Yeah." She laughs. "We made you… you were not

expected, but you were very much wanted. And even though it happened that way, Ellie, you need to know that you are the best thing that has ever happened to me."

I think for a moment. I believe her. Really, I do. It gets quiet again, and more water is crashing on the rocks, and I feel a gentle breeze against my cheeks. "Mom?" I ask.

"Yes, sweetie?"

"If I'm the best thing that ever happened to you, do you think I might be the best thing that could ever happen to my dad?"

She nods. "Yes," she whispers. "I do."

"Do you know where he is?" I ask hopefully.

"Yes, I actually do," she confesses.

"Can I meet him?" I shriek.

She pauses for a beat. "If you would like to," she says.

"Yes!" I say. "Thank you!"

She lifts my sun hat and kisses my forehead. We sit together on the rocks of her special place with the sun shining on our new hats. I have my mom all to myself, and it is the best feeling ever... even better than eating all of the ice cream in the world. And excitement shoots through my veins at the speed of light because I have a feeling, a really good feeling, that I might be getting a dad.

# IN THE PRESENT- HAZEL

## CHAPTER TWENTY-TWO

"She asked what?" Franny's voice pierces through my AirPods.

"She basically implied that she wants to meet her father." I place the bottle of wine into my carriage and continue shopping.

"What did she say exactly?"

"She more or less said that I shouldn't have her all to myself," I say. Of course, those were not her exact words, but I knew what she meant. And she was right.

"What are you going to do?" Franny asks. She is clearly chewing something as she talks to me, and it's difficult to focus on our conversation.

"I don't know yet." I sigh, picking out two steak fillets from the meat counter and adding them to my cart.

"Has he messaged you again?" she asks, obviously referring to Russell Cooper.

"Not since he said he was going out of town."

"Do you think you will meet up with him?" she asks. "He's hot."

I roll my eyes. "I know he's hot, Franny. I'm the one who

had a one-night stand with—" My words are cut short as I turn the corner and see a familiar face shopping in the bread aisle. She looks just as I remember her, although it has been years. She wears a long bright-yellow sundress, and her silver hair is pulled up into a bun. My art teacher from high school—my favorite teacher at that. "Mrs. Davis!" I call, waving at her like a child waves to someone they are excited to see.

She turns and puts her loaf of bread into her basket. She recognizes me immediately. "Oh, Hazel," she says in her adorable British accent. "Hazel Lavigne! How are you, dear?"

"I'm well, thank you."

"It's been years!" She wraps her arms around me for a quick hug.

"Yes, it has," I agree. "I don't think I've seen you since graduation."

"That would make sense," she agrees. "I went back to London soon after your graduation."

"I left for Florida right after graduation."

"What have you been up to since then?"

"I started my own company," I explain. "Events by Hazel. It's down south."

"Oh, how wonderful," she says, clapping her hands together. "Do you still paint?" she asks, her eyes wide and hopeful.

"Not since the painting of the Nubble. I remember that like it was yesterday. Hey, you should come by," I say. "For tea." I smile, remembering how much Mrs. Davis loved her tea. I look through my purse for a pen. "Here, I'll write down the address."

She laughs and pulls her phone out of her purse. "Just text, sweet child," she says.

I laugh and take out my phone. I text her my address and

hug her once more. "I've missed you, Mrs. Davis. I have really missed you."

"I need to run," she explains. "My family is coming to see me at the Anderson Cottage. I am so excited they are visiting."

"That's so nice!" I say. "It was so good to see you, Mrs. Davis," I sing. I smile and turn toward my carriage.

"Oh, dear child." She laughs. "I'm not your teacher anymore. Please call me Emiline."

* * *

LATER THAT EVENING, Warren and I are sitting in the living room of my beach cottage. We have just finished eating the dinner we prepared together, steak fillets with baked sweet potatoes and salad. I don't cook often, so I was relieved when Warren said that I didn't have to cook for him, but I would have to cook with him. I didn't think it was possible to like him more, but I did.

We sit, perched on the couch in the living room of the cottage, our plates empty but our bellies full. We sit together, sipping red wine. I study my date. He wears blue jeans and a button-down short-sleeved shirt. He looks classy; he is classy. I wasn't prepared for the butterflies in my stomach or for my knees to grow weak as a result of his smile, but it's happening. I grin at him and sip my wine as he talks. I can see his lips moving, but his words are lost on me, as all I can think about is how grateful I am that my mother took Ellie for the night.

I cross one leg over and turn to face him, determined to stay engaged in our conversation. I spin my brunette tresses around my finger and continue to smile.

"Do you?" he asks.

I startle, embarrassed that I don't really know exactly

what he is referring to, as my PG-13 Warren fantasy in my mind has turned a bit R-rated. "Do I what?" I ask.

"Do you like dogs?"

"Me? Oh, yes, I love dogs."

"Do you have one?"

"No," I say. "I'm too busy... back home," I confess. "I mean, Gabby could have helped me with the responsibilities but..." My voice trails off.

"Gabby?"

"Yeah," I say, immediately regretting it. "Gabby is... was... my nanny."

He nods, as if understanding, and takes a sip of his wine. "Was?"

"I had to let her go."

"Why?"

"It's kind of a long story."

He smiles and holds the glass to his lips. "I'm not going anywhere," he says and winks.

* * *

HOURS LATER, I have told him the story of Gabby the gambling nanny. We had both laughed, I cried, and we polished off our bottle of wine. We are standing in the kitchen, cleaning up from dinner. I place the last dish in the dishwasher and start it up. "Thank you," I say, smiling. "Thank you for listening... without judgment."

He wraps his arms around my waist and pulls me close to him. He smells delicious. "What is there to judge?" he asks. "You didn't do anything wrong. You're just a mom, trying to do her best."

I stare up at him in wonder. "Where the hell did I find you?" I reach up and kiss his cheek.

"I was going to ask you the same question." We walk back

over to the couch, and he sits down and gestures for me to sit with him. I turn sideways and take a seat on his lap, feeling a bit awkward at first, but when he pulls my legs around his waist and his strong arms seem unyielding, I begin to relax. He pulls me close for a kiss, and any remaining insecurities disappear. The intensity in his kiss makes my knees weak and my heart flutter. His hands cup my backside and pull me closer to him. I trace my hands along the sides of his arms and then squeeze him close to me.

"Want to take this to my bedroom?" I surprise myself by my boldness.

He doesn't answer me with words, but he stands from the couch and swoops me off my feet, carrying me like a groom carries a bride over a threshold. "Which way?" he asks eagerly between kisses.

* * *

I AWAKE in the middle of the night, startled and distressed, from a terrible nightmare. This is something that has happened often since the kidnapping, and I have been unable to shake it. "Ellie!" I gasp. I sit up straight and reach for her, noticing that my hair is a sweaty mess, matted to my damp skin. She isn't there. Of course, she isn't there. She is with my mother. Warren reaches a hand to my naked lower back.

"Are you all right?"

I nod and glance at my cell. 3:00 a.m. My heart continues to race, and I lie back down. Warren pulls me toward him and rests my head against his bare torso, and thoughts from earlier that evening spin through my mind at what feels like a million miles per hour. I can still see the serious concentration in Warren's eyes as he kissed me. I can feel the excitement that ran through my veins as he laid me down on my bed and removed my top. I remember the way I giggled in embarrassment when removing my skinny jeans had not been so effortless. Warren's confidence, however, as he removed his shirt, revealing abs even more perfect than what I imagined, was nothing short of amazing. I smile fondly as I remember how our eyes had locked together and stayed in focus the entire time we made love. We had connected in ways I hadn't expected and experienced such passion that I never knew could be. We must have fallen asleep afterwards, and now hours have gone by, and he was still here... in my bed, something that I never allow to happen, ever.

"I'm good," I lie. "It was a nightmare." I realize that I am not only referring to the bad dream I just had but the entire experience with Ellie and her kidnapping and the dull ache in my gut that seems to always be there, never ceasing.

He pulls me closer to him and moves the blankets over my cold arms and whispers, "You're safe now," and I slowly drift back to sleep, feeling secure and protected in the arms of a man I am pretty sure could be an angel sent from heaven itself.

## IN THE PRESENT- RUSSELL

### CHAPTER TWENTY-THREE

*M*y heart races and beats to the click of my blinker as I exit the highway. West Palm Beach, Florida. Although I only live about an hour from here, I try to avoid it when I can, especially around this time of year. But now, as I drive through the back roads of the outskirts of the city (not the nice ones), my stomach flips again, and part of me considers turning back.

My thoughts are interrupted as my cell phone buzzes on my dash. I swipe it open and answer. "This is Russell."

"Russ, it's Felice. How's it going?"

"Okay," I say to my sister, wondering if she can sense the nervousness in my tone. I can most definitely sense it in hers.

"Are you almost there?"

"Yes," I say, wishing I wasn't almost there. "Don't tell Mom where I am," I remind her for what feels like the hundredth time in twenty-four hours.

She sighs. "How many times do I have to tell you? I'm not saying anything."

"Good," I say. "She doesn't need to worry... and it's just better... that she doesn't know."

"I know."

"What are you going to say to him?"

"I'll probably take him for a drink," I say, knowing that in the big scheme of things, offering him a drink will be the only way he agrees to speak with me.

\* \* \*

LESS THAN TEN short minutes later, I am standing outside of his apartment building. The sun is merciless as it beats down on me, causing the beads of sweat running down my back to multiply by the dozen. I run my hands through the back of my hair, find the name Cooper on the door, and press the button. A loud buzzing sound rings, and seconds later, he answers with a sharp "Hello?"

My knees grow weak, and my stomach flips. I consider turning and walking away. He would never even know I was here. I could hop right back in my car and pretend like he doesn't even exist. After all, isn't that how I have spent the past decade?

I clench my fists by my sides and breathe. "Yes," I say. "Nicky. It's me... Russ."

"Russ?"

"Yes, Russell. Your brother. I need to talk to you... it's really important."

\* \* \*

I COULD SAY he looks like shit, but that would be the understatement of the century. He is younger than me by thirteen months, but now, between his overgrown blond shaggy hairdo and his untamed facial hair that seems to cover his face like a mask, I hardly recognize him. I knew that he wouldn't want to see me, but I also knew that he would come with me if I offered him a free drink at the bar down the street. He ignores me for the entire walk over, puffing on his cigarette like his life depends on it.

"Are you working at all?" I ask. I look around for the bartender, but there is no one in sight.

"Here and there." He avoids making eye contact. His eyes look tired, defeated.

I shake my head, knowing full well that this means no. He is not working, not legally anyways. "Nice," I say, trying not to piss him off.

"What's this about, Russ? I know you didn't come here to see me." He looks at me and smiles, his grin wide and judgmental. "You wrote me off a long time ago," he accuses.

I nod in agreement. "Yeah, Nicky, I did," I admit. "I tried to help you. You didn't want my help." I stare at him through this new exterior and try with all my might to find my brother. But I come up empty. He is lost to addiction, and he has been for years. I stare down at his hands and notice they are shaking, something that used to happen to him often when he started to sober up.

"Look, man, I have some questions for you."

"What, are you a detective now?" he asks, rolling his eyes. "You aren't rolling in dough anymore?"

I sigh and notice a bartender tying an apron around his waist. He approaches us with a smile. "Hey, Nicky," he greets. "Your usual?"

"Not today, Mac," he answers. "My big brother is here to see me, and he's buying."

"Nice!" the bartender exclaims. "So not your usual Budweiser, then?"

"Nope." He chuckles. "My brother here can afford the big bucks."

I roll my eyes. "Don't believe anything this guy says," I say. "I don't make the big bucks."

"Still, we are celebrating here. Screw the Bud... let's make it a vodka sunrise. Two of 'em. For old times' sake."

\* \* \*

ABOUT AN HOUR and a half and a couple of drinks later, my baby brother starts to soften up, and is more than excited to talk to me. I decide that I will take advantage of his change in mood and start my digging. After all, it is why I am here. "Hey, Nick," I start. "When you were a brother at Kappa Beta, do you remember meeting this girl?" I try to keep my tone even and steady, but as I hold the phone up to him and show him a photo of Hazel, he sees right through me.

"Who's asking?" I can't help but notice the change in color. He turns from his normal shade of gray to a deep, sunburned-looking red in a matter of seconds.

"So you know her?" I ask again, holding the photo steady. Hazel smiles up at us from her picture. Her brown hair is pulled back in a ponytail, and her red lipstick makes her teeth look as white as snow. I took a screenshot from her Facebook photos. It had been a picture of her with Ellie, but I cropped the girl out.

"What do you want with that rich bitch?" He grunts.

"So you remember her, then?"

Nick slams his glass on the bar and stands up. "Stay the hell out of it, Russ," he warns. "Just stay the hell out." With that, he walks away, slamming the door behind him, leaving me with two vodka sunrises and all the answers I need.

# IN THE PAST- NICKY 2010

## CHAPTER TWENTY-FOUR

*M*y car was parked across the street from the coffee shop. I pointed my camera in her direction. Click... click... click. I captured her every movement... every smile... each breath. She was seated outdoors at a table with a friend and feeding her infant a bottle. I zoomed in on the baby. Click... click... click. The baby was dressed in a small magenta dress and wrapped in a pink blanket, a girl. A warm feeling shot through me and collided with the darkness of my soul. A thunderstorm of emotions turned my thinking upside down. I immediately closed myself off from feeling it... feeling anything. Hazel smiled at her friend and laughed. I recognized her laugh because she once laughed with me. She once smiled at me. She once wanted me. I really thought we'd hit it off, that night at the frat party. I hadn't meant to sleep with her... okay, maybe I did. But those things happened. And for me, it happened quite often. But this time was different. This time, when it was over, the rumors started. Bastian, the president of our fraternity, had a complaint from one of the Lakeland girls... and they tracked it to me.

"Did you sleep with her, Nicky?" he had asked.

I had thrown my hands up in defense. "Whoa, wait a minute," I argued. "Isn't that what we do here?" I smiled in the charming way I had learned to do back then.

He shoved me up against the wall with one hand. The damn bastard looked little, but he was strong. "That depends, Nicky." His eyes locked onto mine. "Did you do it again?"

"Let me go," I warned. But two other brothers surrounded me on both sides, pinning my arms to the wall.

"I'm going to ask you one more time, Nicky," he spat. "Did you put something in her drink?"

I rolled my eyes. "I mean, no... not technically," I argued. "I put it in *my* drink and let her drink it."

The black eyes they had given me lasted weeks. By the time they were done with me, I was almost unrecognizable. Besides the fact I was excommunicated from the fraternity, I was also kicked off campus and out of school. It was, as some might call it, the beginning of the end for me. I started drinking more, found a whole new gang of drug-addicted friends, and even dabbled in gambling.

So, as I sat there taking photos of Hazel Lavigne and her daughter... my daughter... I wasn't feeling very warm and fuzzy. I placed my camera down on the seat next to me and watched as Hazel stood up from her chair and balanced the baby in one arm and the diaper bag in the other. She turned and walked toward the restroom. This was my cue. I jumped out of my car and jogged across the street to where her friend was seated and sipping her coffee. As I approached the table where the blond-haired friend was sitting, I could see that she was sketching something, a wedding cake perhaps?

"Hey there," I said, pulling back Hazel's chair and sitting at the table.

She looked up, startled, and a bit confused. "Do I know you?" she asked.

"No, but I know you." I spat. "Bitch."

She reached into her purse and pulled out her cell phone. "I'm calling the cops," she warned. "You better get out of here... whoever you are."

I ignored her threat. "You were the one who ratted me out to Bastian Jones," I accused.

She put her phone down on the table and looked at me suspiciously. "Bastian Jones?" she asked, thinking for a moment.

"Yeah," I said firmly. "Ring a bell?"

"Kappa Beta?"

I nodded in agreement and looked over my shoulder. No sign of Hazel. "She wasn't going to tell anyone about what happened. I know it." My voice shook with anger. "You should have let it go." I clenched my fists, aware of the perspiration forming on my palms.

"I know," she agreed. "And she doesn't know I said anything." She paused for a beat. "You put something in her drink, didn't you?"

I slammed my fists on the table, and she jumped back. "She asked you not to tell?" I shouted. "And you ratted me out?"

She bit her lip and nodded. "Yes," she stated firmly. "I know Hazel. She doesn't just sleep with random assholes at frat parties. And I knew if I didn't tell, you would do it again to someone else."

"So now I'm the asshole?" I asked. "She didn't even tell me she was pregnant with my kid, and I'm the asshole? It is mine, right? The baby?"

She nodded again, slowly this time. "But she doesn't know I said anything." Her voice cracked. "Please go away," she begged. "She doesn't need to know about this... about you. She doesn't even remember what you look like. She doesn't want anything from you."

I stood and backed away from the table. "Well, that's a relief because I don't have anything to give. You're going to regret this someday," I hissed. "You ruined my life."

She held my gaze and sipped her coffee. "You better go, whoever you are. Hazel will be back any minute, and I'm about to call the cops."

"Watch your back, Franny." I scowled. I walked away from the table, not looking back even once. I wasn't sure how, but someday, somehow, Hazel and Franny were going to regret what they did to me. *Just wait.*

# IN THE PRESENT- EMILINE

## CHAPTER TWENTY-FIVE

Oh, what a beautiful day this has turned out to be. My daughter, Olivia, and her family have come to visit, along with my son George and his wife, Abigail. Olivia, of course, brought my sweet six-year-old granddaughter, Jenny. I absolutely adore my time with my little Jenny. We are seated at the table in the quaint, cozy kitchen on the third floor of the Anderson Cottage, sipping tea and watching Jenny play with her ponies. She has given them each a name and has decided to call the prettiest one Emiline, after me.

"How are you doing, Mom?" Olivia asks.

"I have good days and bad days," I admit.

"You miss him, don't you?"

I stare over her shoulder at the water on Long Sands Beach. It seemed like yesterday Jason and I were strolling, hand in hand along the shore. It seemed like only seconds ago, he had promised me the world. I fiddle with the promise ring that I wear on my finger, along with my diamond engagement ring. "Of course I miss your father," I say. "I miss him every day."

She nods in agreement. "It's only been a few years," she

says. "Time can heal all things, right?"

I smile at her, thankful that she has remembered my advice over the years, enough to give it back to me. But the truth is, I'm not sure time can heal this broken heart of mine. Jason had been diagnosed with lung cancer back in 2018. He fought long and hard, but in the end, it was his time. When he passed, a piece of my soul died with him. But sitting here now, I am still forever grateful that I allowed myself to fall for him as hard and fast as I did. I grin and think of the famous quote by Alfred Lord Tennyson, "Tis better to have loved and lost than to never have loved at all," and I smile.

George looks up from his cell phone. He has been reading something for a while now. "It will take time, Mom," he reassures.

Jenny jumps up from where she was playing. "Can we go swimming?"

"Soon," Olivia says. "Why don't you go and get your bathing suit on?"

"Okay, Mommy," she sings.

I watch her pull her bathing suit out of her mother's bag and zip into the bathroom to change, and a warm laugh escapes from within. "She is really something," I say. I stare past them again and watch out the window as seagulls fly over the water. They seem to be dancing in the sky, in unison. I think about Jason again and how much he loved it here in York, Maine. After all of the years in London and even after two beautiful children, this is where he had loved to be more than anything. For a while, we made a home of it in York. I taught art at the high school and loved every second of it. But when my mother passed away and my father soon grew ill, we decided to head back to London and take care of him. We raised our children in London and stayed there until both of them graduated high school. It was our plan to travel together once the children were grown, and we did. We traveled all over the globe. But when our children started moving to the States and having babies, we found ourselves rooted in places that would allow us to see them. Oh, Jason loved being a grandfather. His grandchildren could do no wrong. He spoiled them silly.

"We are going to take Jenny to the water," Olivia explains, referring to her and Abby. "Do you want to come?"

"No, child." I say. "You go and have fun. I'll be here."

"Bye, Nana!" Jenny calls. She plants a wet kiss on my cheek. She smells lovely, like Oreo cookies and bubble gum.

"Are you going?" I ask George.

He shakes his head. "No, I'm trying to get to the bottom of something."

He doesn't have to explain. I know for certain that he is worried about his daughter. His oldest daughter, my first grandchild. "She will come around," I say and place my hand on his.

"She misses Dad." He wipes an unexpected tear from his eye. "It all started when Dad died."

"They were like two peas in a pod." I smile, remembering it fondly. The two of them would have picnics and play catch on the beach during our summer visits. Football was their favorite. "She will come around," I say again. "She reminds me a lot of you when you were in your twenties." I laugh. When I look at him, I feel as though I am looking at Jason. The resemblance is uncanny.

"This is different, Mom," he chokes. "I didn't say anything at first... well, because I didn't want to worry you." A slight sob escapes from my son, and for a moment, I am alarmed.

"What is it, dear?" I whisper. My stomach flutters in the same way it did when I got the news of Jason's diagnosis. A small voice in my head whispers, *something is terribly wrong.*

"Gabrielle is in some real trouble this time, Mom... and I don't know how to help her."

## IN THE PRESENT- HAZEL

## CHAPTER TWENTY-SIX

*I* rummage through my beach bag in search of my ringing cell phone. I glance at the unfamiliar number and realize that it is a Florida phone number. I swipe open the screen and place the phone to my ear. "This is Hazel," I say.

"Hazel, my name is Detective Graham Price, calling from the Criminal Investigation Division of Hollywood, Florida, PD." His voice is sharp, with little to no emotion, and his phrases are short. "Ms. Lavigne, is this a good time or a bad time?"

I wave at Ellie and Warren in the distance. He is throwing her the football, and she is catching it. Perfect spirals, just the way she likes it. Ellie waves back to me, her smile consuming her entire face.

"Uh," I stammer. "It's a good time?" I ask more than answer. I adjust my sun hat over my head, readjust my phone to my right ear and block my left ear with my palm. "Is this regarding Gabrielle? Did you find her?" My stomach flips, and I hope to God that they didn't find Gabby dead, as I have gone over many times in my mind since May.

"No, ma'am," he replies. His words are quick and monotone. "We didn't find Gabrielle."

"What is this regarding?"

"Ma'am, we have reason to believe that your daughter might still be in danger."

"I'm sorry, what?" I ask. I jump to my feet and lose my sun hat to the beach breeze. It flies away in Warren's direction.

"Got it!" he calls, referring to my hat.

"What do you mean, in danger?" I shriek.

"Ms. Lavigne, does anyone back home in the state of Florida know your current location?"

"I… uh," I stammer. "Like friends?"

"Yes, ma'am."

"Well, my friend Franny knows where I am. And my assistant Sidone, but I think that's it."

"How about your daughter's father?"

"Russell Cooper? No," I state firmly. "He doesn't know where I am."

"I see." His voice is steady. "Have you posted your location on social media? Facebook, Instagram, Twitter?"

"No," I say. "Given the current situation, I haven't posted anything since May," I respond. "Detective, what is this regarding?"

"Well," he starts, "it appears that Ellie's alleged father had a hunch about your current situation, so he did some digging."

"He's not the alleged father," I correct. "He is Ellie's father."

"The thing is, Russell Cooper has a brother, Nicholas Cooper, who goes by the name Nicky."

My shoulders tighten, and my breath catches in my throat. *Nicky.* The name is familiar. I close my eyes, and I am immediately taken back to that night, the night I gave myself to a stranger on the bottom bunk of the rickety and creaky old bed at the Kappa Beta house. My mind spins, and my knees grow weak. I sit back down in my beach chair and press my face to my knees. I feel like the entire beach is spiraling around me. I remember it clearly, lying on my back while he moved over me, trying desperately to stay awake. Someone came into the room as it was happening. "Damn, Nicky," the guy had exclaimed. "Lock the freaking door next time."

How had I forgotten that? I nod, forgetting that the detective couldn't actually see me.

"Are you there, Ms. Lavigne?"

"Yes, I'm here," I whisper.

"Russell approached his brother about you, and he gets the impression that Nicholas is very much involved in the disappearance of both your daughter and Gabrielle Davis."

"Involved?" My mouth grows dry, and I feel as though I might faint.

"Mommy? Are you okay?"

I look up to see Ellie and Warren standing over me, both looking concerned and worried. Warren hands me my sun hat, and I clutch it to my chest. I try to smile, but I can't. I just shake my head no.

"Take her down to the water Warren, and don't let her out of your sight."

A look of concern washes over Warren's face, but he nods and playfully taps Ellie on the arm. "Race you to the water!" he yells. They run side by side to the shore, Warren giving Ellie a run for her money.

"I'm here," I say into the phone. "Where is he? This Nicky Cooper?"

"We don't have eyes on him yet. That's why I need you to be absolutely sure that he doesn't know your whereabouts."

"I don't believe he does," I say. "Did you question the kidnappers? The ones in custody?"

"They aren't talking. Nobody involved with the Brambrillas usually talks."

"I see," I say, wiping the sweat off my forehead. "So why do you think Nicky is involved?"

"Nicky and his brother Russell look a lot alike. They are very close in age. It is likely that Nicky is the father of your child, not Russell."

"How do you know that?"

"Well, for starters, it appears that Nicky is involved with the Brambrillas. We have him pinged around the city, being seen with quite a few of them. And also, we have witnesses that spotted Nicky and Gabrielle together."

"What?" I gasp.

"That's not all, ma'am," he says. "We have reliable witnesses who say that your daughter was with Gabrielle during one of their meetings. I'm sending over the photograph of Nicky now."

"Ellie," I call. "Come here, please." My voice is shaky, and I think I might throw up. My cell phone dings, and I open the text sent from the detective's phone. I open the photograph, and there, staring back at me, is a mug shot of the man I met back in 2010... Ellie's father. I am sure of it. I can see the resemblance between him and Russell, but this man, this Nicky, looks older... scruffier... dirtier. Nicky is clearly bad news. I try to breathe, but it is becoming more and more difficult.

"Mommy?" Ellie asks, out of breath from running.

"Have you ever met this man?" I show her the photo from my phone.

"What is this about?" Warren asks, crouching down next to me. He places one hand behind my back to steady me and the other on my knee.

"Yeah," Ellie says, looking from me to Warren and back again. "That's Gabby's boss."

"Gabby's boss?" I ask, louder than I mean to. "Who the…"

"Yeah, her boss. You know… for her football job."

"Did you hear that?" I all but shout into my phone. I close my eyes and allow the dizziness to wash over me. The idea of my little girl being exposed to this level of illegal activity is enough to make me lose my mind.

"Yes, ma'am," Detective Price responds. "Sit tight and keep an eye on your daughter. If we are right about this man, he has been planning to get his hands on her for a while now."

I throw my arms up over my head and drop my phone in the sand. Warren picks it up, brushes it off, and hands it back to me. "How do you know that?" I demand into the phone. "What are you not telling me?"

He is quiet for a beat. "Russell received a phone call from a friend of yours," he says with zero emotion in his voice.

"Who?"

"A Francine Gilbert."

"Franny?" I gasp. "What did Franny say?" Why did she call Russell?

"Well, it seems as though back in 2010, she was approached by Nicholas Cooper at a coffee shop."

"She was?" I place my hand over my forehead and shake my head. "She told them about what happened to me at the frat house, didn't she?" I whisper.

"Yes, ma'am," he says. "Nicholas Cooper was kicked out of his fraternity and out of the school. We were able to pull up the records from the university that correlate with her story. Nicholas Cooper approached her and threatened her right after Ellie was born."

"Why wouldn't she tell me?" I cry, tears now falling down my cheeks. "We could have avoided all of it."

"It looks as though she reached out to Russell Cooper, believing him to be the man who approached her the day the two of you were having coffee," he explains. "But it wasn't Russell who approached her. It was Nicholas."

I lean my head on Warren's shoulder, the confusion and concern on his face not going unnoticed. Ellie sits in the sand, looking up at me, her bottom lip quivering like it does right before she starts to cry.

"Where is Franny now?" I ask, suddenly concerned about her. If Nicky was responsible for taking Ellie and involving Gabby, who knows what else he is capable of.

"We are trying to get eyes on her as we speak, Ms. Lavigne."

"I'll try calling her now."

"And, Hazel?" he asks, finally, after this whole conversation, referring to me by my first name.

"Yes?" I ask.

"Do you have any reason to believe that your friend, Francine, could have had anything to do with the kidnapping?"

"No!" I all but shout into my phone. "She may have gone behind my back, but she isn't a kidnapper," I say, sounding annoyed. "If you are suspecting Franny, you are way off."

"Okay," he says. "Just one more thing..." His voice trails off.

*I don't know how much more of this I can take*, I think. "What is it?" I ask.

"We questioned Bastian Jones, from the fraternity," he says.

"Who is Bastian Jones?" I ask.

"He was the president of the fraternity, back on your, um... date of conception," he says awkwardly.

"Okay?"

"He reports that Nicky had a history of slipping girls GHB during frat parties... and he has reason to believe that you were drugged too."

I swallow and hold my breath for a beat, turning away from Warren. Of course, this confirms something that I have always considered in the back of my mind but never really wanted to come to terms with. "Thank you for letting me know." I hang up the phone and fall into Warren's arms. I allow him to hold me and comfort me as I cry. Ellie wraps her arms around my waist, and the three of us stay together, in an embrace that lasts minutes but feels like hours.

"Are you okay?" Warren asks.

I shake my head. "It isn't good," I whisper back.

"It's going to be okay," he reassures and kisses my forehead softly.

I reach up and kiss his cheek. "Thank you," I say, never wanting to let him go. "I have to call Franny," I say. "She's probably freaking out."

"Okay." He kisses my cheek and holds me tighter.

"And I need to figure out how to get a paternity test."

"One thing at a time," Warren says.

"Thank you," I say, "for helping me through this."

"Thank you for letting me."

* * *

ABOUT AN HOUR LATER, we are back at my cottage. Ellie is taking a shower, and Warren is preparing dinner. I can't even begin to think about eating. I sit on my couch, still in my bathing suit and sundress, drinking water and dialing Franny's number. I know, deep down in my heart, that she didn't mean to hurt me. I suppose I also knew that Franny wouldn't let the frat guy who drugged and impregnated me get away with it.

She answers on the second ring. "Hazel?" she asks. "Are you okay?"

"Yeah," I reply. "We are okay."

"Good," she responds. "There is something I have to tell you." I can hear the crack in her voice, and I know the shakiness means she is trying not to cry.

"I already know everything."

"You do?"

"Yes."

"I'm so sorry," she cries. "If I had said something sooner..." Her voice trails off.

"You did what you thought was right. It's okay."

"Russell Cooper," she says. "He's a really great guy, you know?"

"He seems like it." I cringe, a part of me still grieving the fact that he is not, in fact, Ellie's dad. Instead, I have passed him up for a gambling, kidnapping criminal.

"When I called him and asked him about the day at the coffee shop," she says, "he didn't know what I was talking about... I think he knew right then that it was his brother."

"Then it makes sense," I say. "Franny, is there anything else you need to tell me? The detective, he wanted to know if you could have been involved. I told him no, obviously." I laugh my nervous laugh, and she is silent for a moment.

"That's all of it," she says. And I believe her. "I told Bastian about you, and I told him that you weren't the kind of girl to sleep around. He had mentioned to me that Nicky had been slipping girls GHB. The frat house was under a microscope with the university because it wasn't the first time. Russell said that Nicky blames you and me for his shitty life." She is crying harder now. "I never meant to hurt anyone... especially you and Ellie."

I lie back down on the couch and close my eyes. "I know, Franny." I think about Franny and how she was my number one supporter back then. She was always trying so hard to protect me... to protect Ellie. It makes sense now. "Franny," I say, thinking out loud. "Remember when we decided to hire a nanny?"

"Yeah." She laughs. "You kept forgetting to pick your kid up at day care."

I roll my eyes. "Yeah," I say. "How did we find Gabby? I was trying to think about it, and I can't remember."

"Remember... Facebook had started becoming popular right around then. I posted something to your immediate friends, and we got a few hits."

"That's right," I say. "But if Gabby wasn't a friend of mine, it would need to be a mutual friend, correct?"

"I guess that makes sense."

I place her on speaker phone and click on my Facebook page, wondering why I hadn't thought to do this before. Had I been too preoccupied and too focused on Events by Hazel to even check the nanny's references?

"What are you doing?" she asks.

"I'm on Gabby's Facebook."

"What are you looking for?"

"I don't know," I admit. "I'm just wondering if there is any connection here, in our mutual friends... you know, like maybe the Coopers or someone who had to do with the kidnapping, like the Brambrillas."

"Huh," she says. "I'm pretty sure Nicky Cooper isn't on social."

I laugh. "You're probably right." I click on our mutual friends anyway, just to see. I stop suddenly, needing to check the name I see before me. "That's crazy," I say.

"What's crazy?"

"My art teacher from high school. She's a mutual friend of Gabby and me."

"Really?" she asks. "That is weird."

"Even weirder," I say. "She is in town... I just saw her a

couple of weeks ago." I click on the profile for Emiline Davis and scroll through her photos.

"Gabby Davis," I say. "Emiline Davis... I mean, it's a common last name, but I should have picked up on the commonality." I click past photos of Emiline and her family, and one catches my eye in particular. It is stunning. It is her with her late husband. They are sitting on the rocks in front of the Nubble. Her silver hair is pulled up in a twist, and he is standing behind her with his arms wrapped around her waist. It is titled "Where we first met." I continue clicking by and finally come across a post she made about a year ago. It is her husband Jason and Gabby. Gabby looks to be about Ellie's age in this picture. Gabby is perched on Jason's lap, and she is holding a football. The post reads, "Happy Birthday to my Gabby. Nana and Grandpa love you."

"Franny." I gasp.

"What is it?"

"My art teacher from high school, Mrs. Davis, is Gabby's grandmother... how did I miss this?"

"And you said she is there? In York?"

"She was. At least a couple of weeks ago she was," I say. "Hey, I will call you later, okay?"

"Okay," she says. "Hazel?"

"I know, Franny. I love you too," I say, hanging up the phone.

"Hey, Warren," I call to the kitchen. "Will you watch Ellie? I'm driving over to the Anderson Cottage. There is someone I need to see."

# IN THE PRESENT- EMILINE

## CHAPTER TWENTY-SEVEN

My hands shake as I cut the Italian bread. The knife slices through it easily, with little effort, but my arthritis has started acting up again, which is a shame, as I do still love to paint. My dinner company is arriving shortly. I marvel at the three place settings on my little table of the Anderson Cottage. I do love it here. So many memories, so many happy memories.

There is a knock at the door, and I open it, thankful that they have arrived on time. My, am I hungry! But the person on the other side of the door is not who I expect it to be. She stands there, Hazel Lavigne, her brown hair up in a messy bun, and she wears a green sundress.

"Hazel," I say. "What a pleasant surprise… do come in!"

She walks inside the cottage and notices my table. "Oh, I'm sorry," she says. "You are having company?"

"Yes, dear. Any moment now."

"I should have called first," she says. "I can come back another time."

"Nonsense," I say. "Have a seat." I gesture to the sofa, and she sits down, wrapping her sundress over her knees.

"What brings you here?"

She hesitates for a moment, and when she starts to speak, I can sense a bit of worry in her tone. "Your granddaughter," she says. "Gabby Davis."

I sit back, startled, and for a moment, I am caught off guard. "You know my Gabby?" I ask.

She nods. "Yes."

"How?"

"Gabby was the nanny I hired for my daughter, Ellie... just about nine years ago."

*Good heavens, no*, I think to myself. My George told me that Gabrielle had gotten herself into some trouble and ended up helping some loan sharks take a poor little girl from school. Judging by her face, I don't need to explain this to Hazel. "I'm so sorry," I say. "I know it's no excuse for what you've been through, but Gabby... she has been so lost since her grandfather passed away. When he passed, a piece of her did too. Why, she didn't even come to the funeral because she had to work..." My voice trails off, and I realize that she didn't come to the funeral because she was babysitting Hazel's daughter.

"Have you spoken to her?" Hazel asks. "I'm asking because I'm worried about her."

"Oh, heavens child! I'm worried about her too."

"So, you haven't spoken to her?"

"I'm afraid not."

"They haven't found her yet," Hazel explains. "She really got in over her head this time."

I nod. "You can say that again."

"Could you let me know if you hear from her?"

"Of course, I will."

She stands to leave, but there is a knock on the door.

"It's my company," I say.

"I'll get out of your way," she says.

"Nonsense," I say. "It's just my friends from downstairs. They would love to meet you, I'm sure." I holler for them to come in, and they do. "Cassidy and Sean, this is my former student, Hazel Lavigne."

Cassidy enters the cottage and places a large ceramic bowl on my counter. Sean follows behind and sets a large pot on the stove. I can smell those delicious meatballs from a mile away. Cassidy's red hair is braided; her sun-kissed blond highlights peek through and brighten up her face... if it's possible for her face to be any brighter. Ever since she met that Sean Anderson, she has seemed nothing but happy. Her green eyes shine. "Hi," she sings. "I'm Cassidy, and this is my fiancé, Sean."

Sean walks over to Hazel and shakes her hand. "Sean," he states. "Sean Anderson." He runs his hand through his dark hair and smiles.

"Hazel," she says. "Nice to meet you."

"Those meatballs smell amazing," I say. "Hazel, won't you stay a bit? Try some of Cassidy's famous meatballs?"

"I wish I could," she politely declines. "My... Warren... is making dinner," she says awkwardly. "Your ring is beautiful," she says to Cassidy.

"Oh, thank you," Cassidy says. "It's been in my... our family... for years." She looks up at Sean, and he smiles. He is such a handsome boy. I wish I could squeeze those dimples of his.

"When's the wedding?" Hazel asks.

"We haven't set a date yet," she explains. "But we are in the process of choosing our location. We are either having it at the Union Bluff Hotel or the Nubble."

"Both places are breathtaking," Hazel exclaims. "I bet you will have a lovely wedding."

"Hazel is an event planner," I brag. "She has a big company down in Florida."

Hazel smiles and nods. "Yes, Mrs. Davis, I do."

"Emiline," I correct.

"Yes, Emiline," she says, smiling.

"Will you be in town long?" Cassidy asks her, her eyes wide. "I'm an attorney, and Sean is a writer. Neither of us are great with wedding details. It would be so nice to pick your brain."

"Sure, I would love to help. Emiline has my phone number," she says. "It was very nice to meet you both. I will leave you to your dinner. Thank you for speaking with me tonight, Emiline."

"I will keep you posted, dear," I say. "I will keep you posted."

She exits the cottage, and a sense of sadness washes over me.

"Are you okay?" Cassidy asks.

I pull her close to me in a tight embrace. "I will be, child, thank you."

"How about some meatballs?" Sean calls from the kitchen. "I hear they make everything better."

I laugh. "Yes, please," I say, thankful for my dear friends and their company.

CHAPTER TWENTY-EIGHT

"What are you thinking about?" Warren asks. He is seated on my sofa, and I am lying down. I am using his lap as a pillow. He stares down at me and traces my cheek with his fingers.

"Everything," I admit. "I'm worried about Gabby, but I'm also so angry with her."

Warren leans down and kisses my forehead. "How was your visit… to the Anderson Cottage?"

"It was good. I met the couple who live on the second floor, Cassidy and Sean. They are really nice."

"I know Sean," he says. "Sean Anderson, right?"

"Yes, that's right. How do you know him?"

"He taught a writing workshop at the school this past spring. He published a book," he says, thinking for a minute. "I can't remember the title, but it was based on true events… something that happened with his grandfather and his fiancée's grandmother." He grabs his phone and types into the search engine. "Here," he says, showing me a picture of the book, revealing a photograph of the Nubble Lighthouse. The sky in the photograph contains wisps of pink and purple. The lighthouse stands tall against the night sky. "It's called *Stories of the Nubble Light*," he explains. "The kids in Luke's Literature class went nuts over it."

"Good for him," I say. "I'll have to read it." I smile up at him. "Have you talked to Lucas about... us?" I ask awkwardly.

"You mean like, did I ask his permission?" He laughs. "Nope. The way I see it, you snooze, you lose." He is ridiculously handsome. I run my fingers along his dark skin and smile.

"I almost called you my boyfriend today," I say, giggling at my own remark.

"When?" he asks, sounding amused.

"When I was talking to Emiline and her guests." I cover my face with my hands. "I went to say my boyfriend... but I changed it to... my Warren." I laugh.

He pauses for a moment and turns serious. "Can I be your boyfriend?" he asks. His voice sounds smooth and steady.

"I don't know," I joke. "It's a pretty big job."

He leans down and kisses my lips. "Someone's got to do it."

I kiss him again, and this time, it is a longer, more passionate kiss. "Fine," I say, pulling back. "You can be my boyfriend."

"Excellent," he whispers.

I kiss him again, and I run my fingers through his hair. His fingers trace over my neck, collarbone, and down to my chest. For a moment, I feel like the luckiest woman alive. There is a glimmer of hope inside me, and a little voice in the back of my head whispers that I am going to be okay.

"Mommy!" Ellie calls from the stairs. Both Warren and I jump up straight, like two teenagers being caught in a compromising position. I adjust my sundress and walk over to the stairs where my daughter is standing, holding her cell phone. "Mommy, it's Franny," she says, handing me her cell phone. I take her phone from her, confusion washing over me.

"Franny?" I say into Ellie's phone.

"I tried calling you, but you didn't answer."

"Oh. What's going on?" I walk back into the kitchen where my cell phone has been sitting on the charger. Three missed calls from Franny and two from Detective Price. "Shit," I say. "What did I miss?"

"It's over!" she exclaims.

"What?" I ask. I open the text message from Detective Price and see that he has sent me two mug shots. One of Nicky and one of Gabby. Nicky looks even worse than he had in the previous photograph. The thought of him being my daughter's father is enough to make me want to puke. Gabby looks horrible as well. Her once bleach-blond curly hair has been dyed jet black. The bags underneath her eyes and the look of shame on her face all but break my heart.

**Detective Price:** Please confirm that this woman was your nanny.

I TRY to type back quickly, but my fingers are shaking.

**Hazel:** Yes, that is her. Sorry I missed this text.

"THEY HAVE Nicky Cooper in custody, and they have Gabby," Franny repeats.

"Where was she?" I ask Franny, noticing that the room around me is starting to spin, like a carousel at the amusement park.

"She was staying with Nicky. Apparently, after Russell

went to see him, they fled the area. They found them both outside of Miami. By the way, Gabby looks like shit, right? But it's over, Hazel. It's really over!"

My knees weaken, and I drop to the floor, immediately starting to sob uncontrollably.

"What is it, Mommy?" Ellie asks. She's down at my feet, her hands on my knees. "Gabby?" she asks.

Warren scoops up Ellie in one arm and pulls me up with his free hand, bringing me close.

"Gabby is okay." I sob. "Gabby is okay."

* * *

A FEW HOURS LATER, Ellie is tucked in bed and sound asleep. It is getting late, and this was the longest day ever. Warren and I share a bottle of wine and wait for my parents to arrive. I had called my mother to tell her the news, and she was over-the-moon excited. She asked if she and Dad could come over and meet Warren. Although I was eager for alone time with him, I didn't have it in my heart to say no. Warren had joked that this was moving rather fast. He committed to our exclusivity and, on the same night, was meeting the parents. His sense of humor was a breath of fresh air in an otherwise chaotic situation.

I had also called Emiline Davis, as I wasn't sure if her son would have been notified of Gabby's apprehension.

"I just hung up the phone with my Georgie," she had said. "I'm so sorry this happened," she cried between tears. "But I'm glad she is all right."

"Yes," I had whispered back. "Maybe now she can get the help that she needs?"

"Let's hope so," she said. "And Hazel?"

"Yes?"

"You mentioned someone by the name of Warren earlier, yes?"

"Yes," I said. "He is someone that I am... well, seeing."

"Would you mind some advice from an old lady?" she asked. Her tone changed from melancholy to a bit more hopeful.

"Sure."

She spoke slowly and clearly, and I hung on to every word. "Don't hesitate," she instructed.

"Don't hesitate?" I asked, a bit confused.

"Love him, Hazel. Love him like it is the most important thing you will ever do." Her voice was soft like a whisper. "'Tis better to love and lost than to never have loved at all. Love him... love all of him, and the memories you make together will keep you feeling alive, even when your story must come to an end."

\* \* \*

THERE's a knock on the door, and my parents enter, my mother carrying a cake of some sort and a bottle of wine.

"Hi, Mom."

Her eyes meet mine briefly but focus directly on Warren. She winks at me in approval. "Hot stuff," she whispers, loud enough for him to hear it.

"Mom!" I scold.

"Hey, honey," my dad says as he enters the cottage. "I hear we get to celebrate tonight."

I laugh. "Yeah, didn't you hear? It's the 'congratulations, your daughter's kidnapping, biological father is behind bars, and your gambling, addicted nanny has been found alive and well' celebration."

My mother rolls her eyes and extends her hand to Warren. "Hi, I'm Beverly," she says. "Beverly Lavigne."

"Warren Green," he says, shaking her hand in return.

"Donald," my father says. "You can call me Don."

"Nice to meet you, Don," Warren says to my father. "Can I get you a glass of wine?"

"Absolutely," he says. "That would be great."

"So, you and Hazel," my dad says awkwardly as Warren unscrews the cork from the bottle. "You are, what, going steady?"

"Dad!" I interrupt. "Leave Warren alone. I kind of like this one." I wrap my arm around Warren's waist and pull him close to me.

"I'm okay." Warren laughs and kisses my cheek.

"I remember young love," my dad says, pouring the wine into our glasses. "The first time I laid eyes on your mother, I knew she was the one."

I roll my eyes. "Here we go," I warn. "Between her luminous brunette hair and her angelic acoustic guitar, dad all but couldn't control himself," I mock.

"Don't forget her hazel eyes," Dad adds. "Why do you think we named you Hazel?"

"I know." I laugh. "You fell in love with Mom's hazel eyes on the night you met." I take Warren's hand in mine and smile, thinking that maybe, just maybe, I could be with this man forever.

* * *

LATER THAT EVENING, after my parents had gone, Warren and I are snuggled up together in my bed. My back is pressed up against him, and his arms surround me in a soothing embrace. It's funny how much can happen in such a short amount of time. Just this past May, I was running around like a chicken with my head cut off, putting Events by Hazel at the forefront of my life, and now I am back home... a place where I didn't think I wanted to be, surrounded by people I didn't think I needed... or even needed me. How wrong had I been? I need my parents and my family so much, and my baby girl needs me.

I close my eyes and wonder, what is next for Ellie and me? We could head back to Florida, and I could pick up the pieces of my company. I would have to promote Sidone, of course. She was the glue that held Events by Hazel together while I was gone. And of course, Franny needs me. Although, judging by what she had said to me over text this evening, I'm not too sure she needs me as much as she once did.

**Franny:** So... Russell Cooper... now that he isn't Ellie's baby daddy, would you mind if I went out with him? He's VERY easy on the eyes.
**Hazel:** OMG. Of course not. Just steer clear of his brother. (Scared emoji)
**Franny:** (Thumbs-up emoji) And, Hazel? I love you.
**Hazel:** Ditto

I SMILE TO MYSELF, thankful and happy with the fact that Franny might have found someone. Warren pulls me closer against him and kisses the back of my neck. "What are you thinking about?" he whispers in the darkness. I can't see him, but I can feel the beat of his heart against my back. The heat from his whisper is electrifying.

"You. I'm thinking about you, Warren Green."

I turn so I can face him, and he wraps his arms around my waist. I lean in and kiss his lips, and I allow myself to escape from all of my thoughts, all of my worries, and all of my fears.

"What about me?" he asks. A speck of moonlight sneaks through my window, allowing me to see his smile.

"Your smile," I whisper. "It feels like... like home."

He scoops me on top of him with little effort and kisses me again. "I love you, Hazel Lavigne."

Excitement races through my veins at the speed of light. "I love you too," I say. I kiss the top of his forehead and squeeze him against me again. "Warren?" I say in the darkness. "It's really nice to be home."

He rolls on top of me and surrounds my body with kisses. I close my eyes and surrender to the intense passion we share, and I smile to myself, knowing that even though I went through hell and back to get to this place, this is where I am meant to be.

# IN THE FUTURE

## EPILOGUE

$\mathcal{I}$ stand at the door in anticipation. After all, I have only waited my entire life for this night. Everything is perfect, what I have always imagined it would be, knowing that now, after all this time, *I* will be the one smiling in the pictures, and *I* will be the one dancing in the spotlight. It is nothing short of a dream come true. I have envisioned it many times, my arms wrapped around him tightly, our feet moving together in unison to my favorite song. I can imagine the smiles on their faces as they watch in admiration, knowing that happily ever after does exist. I know because I am living it. I have sat back and watched, time after time, other people living their dreams. So it seems only right that now, after all this time, it is my turn to live, my turn to love.

I PRESS my lips together and close my eyes. My stomach flips and flops, and my heart races, faster and faster like a beat of a drum, picking up at a steady pace and building dynamically. Any minute now, I will open the door. I will step over the threshold, and he will be on the other side. He will take my hand in his. He will smile in that familiar way he does, nothing short of perfect.

The night won't last forever, and this saddens me. But when the last song ends and the dance floor clears, it will be only the beginning.

"Are you ready?" Mommy asks. She waits eagerly with her cell phone out in front of her.

"Are you going to video?" I ask, a bit annoyed.

"Of course." She laughs. She stands behind me, at the stairs of our York home. Her brown hair hangs down over her shoulders, and her smile is huge.

The doorbell rings, and we both jump.

"You look beautiful," she says. "Open the door. He is waiting."

I open the front door, and standing there before me is my dad. He is wearing a gray suit with a pink shirt underneath. His pink shirt matches my dress, just as he had promised. He extends a bouquet of pink roses, my favorite.

"Pink roses!" I exclaim. I can't help it. I jump up and down.

"How did I get the prettiest date in the entire sixth grade?" he asks as he enters the house.

"Thank you for the flowers," I say again.

"I'll take those and put them in water for you," Mom offers.

My dad leans forward and kisses her on the lips. She pulls back and stares into his eyes. "You're a handsome man, Warren Green," she says. "You two are going to be the best-looking couple at the father-daughter dance, for sure," she says, her eyes bright.

"Thank you, Mrs. Green," he responds, kissing her hand. "You're pretty good-looking yourself."

My dad reaches down and takes my hand and kisses it

too. I get butterflies in my stomach. "Is my date ready for a fun night?" he asks.

"Yes!" I squeal.

"I forgot to video," Mom cries. "Here, let me at least get a picture."

I lean against my father and smile, the biggest smile I have ever shown.

"Have fun!" she says. "Take more pictures!"

"Okay," I say as I wave goodbye to my Mom, my friend. I wrap my small arm around my father's, and we walk outside, hand in hand. Not just into the perfect sunset but into a life full of love and a future full of promise... just as I have always planned.

# ABOUT THE AUTHOR

Stacy Lee is the author of the Nubble Light Series. Stacy is a lifelong resident of New England. She lives in New Hampshire with her incredibly supportive husband, two beautiful children, and two well loved (spoiled) rescue pups. She enjoys spending time in the beautiful and historic town of York Beach, Maine with her family. The Nubble Lighthouse holds a special place in her heart.

Before she started writing women's fiction, Stacy received her bachelor's degree in elementary education with a teacher certification in grades K-8. She taught elementary school and writing courses to students for fourteen years while completing a graduate degree in elementary administration where she graduated with honors. After that, ( in an effort to drive her husband completely crazy) decided to switch careers and go to Bible College, where she graduated with a Master's in Christian Ministry with a focus in Homiletics.

Finally, when she got tired of taking college courses she decided to do the two things that make her happiest-working for her family business with her best friend and writing. She is thankful for her husband and his ability to bring out the best in her...always.

ALSO BY STACY LEE

COMING SOON!


## The Nubble Light Series Book # 3
## Never in a Billion

*What if your soulmate was off limits?*

Never in a Billion is a story of friendship, love, devotion, and
friendship. As a young teen, Maggie Thatcher's lifestyle left much to
be desired with low self-esteem and a rebellious attitude as her
signature characteristics. After getting caught up with the wrong
crowd, Maggie found herself sentenced to community service hours
at a local retirement facility in Wells, Maine, where she was
introduced to a young man who forever changed her life. During
her time at Wells Village Cove Retirement and Senior Living
Center, Maggie encountered countless individuals whose stories
influenced her to thrive and mature in ways she never imagined
possible. Now Maggie is a successful career woman who has
everything she has ever wanted. Everything, that is, except the one
man she desires. As Maggie gets a front row seat into the lives of
people she once knew as strangers, Maggie learns that we are all
connected in one way or another—even in ways we could never
imagine.

Made in the USA
Columbia, SC
18 February 2022